Amélie Rives

A Brother to Dragons

And Other Old-Time Tales

Amélie Rives

A Brother to Dragons
And Other Old-Time Tales

ISBN/EAN: 9783337072223

Printed in Europe, USA, Canada, Australia, Japan

Cover: Foto ©Andreas Hilbeck / pixelio.de

More available books at **www.hansebooks.com**

A BROTHER TO DRAGONS

AND

OTHER OLD-TIME TALES

BY

AMÉLIE RIVES

AUTHOR OF "THE QUICK OR THE DEAD?" "THE WITNESS OF THE SUN,"
"VIRGINIA OF VIRGINIA," ETC.

COPYRIGHT

LONDON

GEORGE ROUTLEDGE AND SONS

BROADWAY, LUDGATE HILL

GLASGOW, MANCHESTER, AND NEW YORK

1889

PREFACE.

Of the tales published in this volume, "A Brother to Dragons" appeared in the *Atlantic Monthly* for March, 1886; "The Farrier Lass o' Piping Pebworth" in *Lippincott's Magazine* for July, 1887; and "Nurse Crumpet tells the Story" in *Harper's Magazine* for September, 1887.

Amélie Rives.

CONTENTS.

A BROTHER TO DRAGONS.

I.

In the year of grace, 1586, on the last day of the month of May, to all who may chance to read this narrative, these:

I will first be at the pains of stating that had it not been for Marian I had never indited these or any other papers, true or false. Secondly, that the facts herein set down be true facts; none the less true that they are strange. I will furthermore explain that Marian is the Christian name of my lawful wife, and that our surname is Butter.

My wife had nursed the Lady Margaret from the moment of her birth; and here I must make another digression. The Lady

I

Margaret was the twin sister of the then
Lord of Amhurste, Lord Robert, and my
lady and his lordship had quarrelled—Marian saith, with a great cause, but I cannot
herein forbear also expressing my opinion,
which is to the effect that for that quarrel
there was neither cause, justice, nor reason.   Therefore, before those who may
chance to read these words, I will lay bare
the facts pertaining to the said quarrel.

It concerned the family ghost, which
ghost was said to haunt a certain blue
chamber in the east wing of the castle.
Now I myself had never gainsaid these
reports; for although I do not believe in
ghosts, I have a certain respect for them, as
they have never offered me any affront, either by appearing to me or otherwise mal-
treating me.   But Marian, who like many
of her sex seemed to consort naturally with
banshees, bogies, apparitions, and the like,
declared to me that at several different and
equally inconvenient times this ghost had

presented itself to her, startling her on two occasions to such an extent that she once let fall the contents of the broth-bowl on Herne the blood-hound, thereby causing that beast to maliciously devour two breadths of her new black taffeta Sunday gown; again, a hot iron wherewith she was pressing out the seams of Lady Margaret's night-gown. On the second occasion, she fled along the kitchen hall, shrieking piteously, and preceded by Doll, the kitchen wench, the latter having in her seeming a certain ghostly appearance, as she was clad only in her shift, which the draughts in the hall inflated to a great size. The poor maid fled affrighted into her room and locked the door behind her; yet when I did essay to assuage the terror of Mistress Butter, identifying Doll and the blue-room ghost as one and the same, she thanked me not, but belabored me in her frenzy with the yet warm iron, which she had instinctively snatched up in her flight; demanding of me at the same

time if I had ever seen Doll's nose spout
fire, and her eyes spit in her head like hot
coals. I being of a necessity compelled to
reply "No," Marian further told me that it
was thus that the ghost had comported itself; that, moreover, it was clad all in a livid
blue flame from top to toe, and that it had
a banner o' red sarcenet that streamed out
behind like forked lightning. She then
said that this malevolent spirit had struck
her with its blazing hand, and that, did I
not believe her, I could see the burn on
her wrist. Upon my suggesting that this
wound might have been inflicted by the
iron in its fall, she did use me in so un-
wifely a manner that I sought my bed in
much wrath and vexation of spirit. Nay,
I do fear me that I cursed the day I was
wed, the day on which my wife was born,
wishing all women to the d—l; and that,
moreover, out loud, which put me to much
shame afterwards for some days; although,
be it said to my still greater shame, it was

full a fortnight e'er I confessed my repentance unto the wife whom I had so
abused.

But meseems I have in this digression
transgressed in the matter o' length; therefore, to return to the bare facts.

It was on the subject of this ghost that
my lord and the Lady Margaret had dis-
agreed. My lord, being a flighty lad, although a marvellous fine scholar and well-
disposed, did agree with my wife in the
matter of the ghost; while my lady was of
a like mind with myself.

It doth seem but yesterday that she came
to me as I was training the woodbine o'er
the arbor that led to her little garden, and
put her white hand on my shoulder. (My
lady was never one for wearing gloves, yet
the sun seemed no more to think o' scorch-
ing her fair hands than the leaves of a day-
lily.) She comes to me and lays her hand
on my shoulder, and her long eyes they
laugh at me out of the shadow of her hat;

but her mouth is grave as though I were a
corse.

Quoth she:

"Butter, dost thou believe in this ghost?"

"Nay, my lady," answered I, hoping to
shift her to better soil; "I ne'er meddle
with ghosts or goblins. Why, an there be
such things, should they wish me harm?
O' my word, my brain is no more troubled
with ghosts, black or white, than our gracious Queen's"—here I doffed my cap—
"is with snails and slugs;" and here I
plucked a slug from a vine-leaf and set
my heel on't.

"Nay, nay!" quoth she, a-shutting of her
white eyelids so tight that all the long black
hairs on them stood straight out, like the
fringe on Marian's Sunday mantle in a
high wind. "Butter! thou nasty man!"

"Why—for how dost thou mean, my
lady?" quoth I.

"Why, for mashing that poor beast to
a pap." And then a-holding of her hand

level below her eyes, so that she might not discern the ground, "Is he dead?" quoth she.

"Dead?" asked I, for I was somewhat puzzled in my mind.

"Ay, the slug; is he dead?"

"That he is, verily," said I; for in truth he was naught but a jelly, and therewith I drew a pebble over him with my foot, that the sight o' his misfortune should not disturb her tender heart.

"How if I were to crush you 'neath my heel, Master Butter?" quoth she at last, having peered about for the sight she dreaded, and, not seeing it, returning to her discourse. "How wouldst thou like that, excellent Master Butter?" But somehow, as I looked at her foot, my mouth, for all I could do, went into a smile. For though she was as fine a maiden as any in all Warwickshire, her foot, methinks, was of so dainty a make 'twould scarce have dealt death to a rose.

"But truly, my lady," continued I, seeing that she was making up a face at me,
"thou knowest I've naught in common with
ghosts."

"Ay," quoth she. "And thou knowest
the like of me. But"—and here stops she,
with the slyest tip of her frowzed curls towards the house—"thou knowest also this,
Butter, that his lordship, my brother, thinks
as doth Marian, thy wife, and that therein
we four cannot agree."

So I look at my hoe-handle, and say I,
"My lady, it is known to me."

"Well, now, Butter," she goes on, "thou
most wise, most excellent, most cunning,
most delectable of Butters, I have con-
cocted a plan. I' fecks, Butter" (for my
lady, like her Majesty the Queen, was somewhat given to swearing, though more mod-
est oaths, as should become a subject)—
"I' fecks, Butter," saith she, "'t is a most
lustick plot. But I would not thy mome
heard us;" and with that she makes me

send away Joe, the under-gardener. He being gone, she whispers in my ear how she hath plotted to fright his lordship and Marian into very convulsions of further conviction, by appearing to them at the door o' the blue room in her night-gown, with a taper in her hand and her face chalked. What she desired o' me was, that I should come to the blue room with her, and there remain while she played off this pretty fantasy on my lord and Marian.

To be truthful in these my last days o' earth, I liked not my proffered office o'er-well. Howbeit, that night did I do the bidding o' my young mistress, and—loath am I to speak of it, even at this late day—'twas the cause of my young master's leaving his home and going to bide in foreign countries.

Ah, bitter tears did his sister weep, and with mine own eyes I saw her, on the day he set forth, cling to his neck, and when he shook her thence, hang about his loins, and when at last he pushed her to the ground, she laid her hands about his feet and wept; and between every sob it was, "Go not, brother, for my fault! Go not, brother, for my fault!" or else, "Robin, Robin, dost not love me enough to forgive me so little?" and then, "If thou didst but love me a little, thou couldst forgive me much." But he stepped free of her hands and went his ways, and my lady lay with her head where his feet had been, and was still.

Then Marian, who was very wroth with me for my part in the matter, did up with her nursling in her own proper strong arms (for she was aye a strong lass, that being one o' the chief reasons for which I had sought her in marriage—having had, as should all men, an eye to my posterity. It was a great cross to me, as may be thought, to find that all my forethought had been in vain, and that while Turnip, the farrier, had eight as fine lads as one would care to father, of a puny wench that my Marian could have slipped in her pocket, Mistress Butter presented me with no children, weakly or healthy). But, as I have said, Marian, in her own arms, did carry my lady up-stairs to her chamber, and laid her on the day-bed.

And by-and-by she opes her eyes (for Marian agreed that I sate on the threshold), and says she, putting out her hand half-fearful-like, " Is't thou, brother?"

" Nay, honey," saith Marian; " it is I, thy Marian, thy nurse."

Then said my lady, " Ay, nurse; but my brother, he is below — is't not so?" But when Marian shook her head, my lady sate up on the day-bed and caught hold of her short curls, and cried out, " I have banished him! I have made him an outlaw! I have banished him!" And for days she lay like one whose soul was sped.

Well, the young lord came not back, nor would he write; so we knew not whether he were alive or dead. Yet were Marian

and myself not unhopeful, for full oft did
the heady boy find some such cause of dis-
agreement with his sister to abide apart
from her.   But when we saw that in truth
he came not back, and that week sped
after week, and month did follow month,
and still no tidings, we had perforce to ac-
knowledge that the young lord was indeed
gone to return no more.

The Lady Margaret, in her loneliness,
grew into many strange ways.   She did
outride any man in the county, and she had
a blue-roan by the name of Robin Hood;
which same, methinks, no man in or out o'
th' county would 'a' cared to bestride.   She
would walk over to Pebworth ('piping Pebworth,' as Master Shakespeare hath dubbed
it) and back again, a distance o' some six
miles; and afterwards set forth for a gallop
on Robin Hood, and be no more a-weary,
come eventide, than myself from a trip
'round the gardens.   She swam like a sea-
maid, she had fenced even better than her

brother, and methinks she was the bonni-
est shot with a long-bow of any woman in
all England. She was but fifteen when
my lord left Amhurste for aye, and in the
years since she had grown mightily, and
was waxed as strong as Marian, and full
a head taller. But she had long, curved
flanks that saved her from buxomness;
and her head was set high· and light on
her shoulders, like a bird that floats on
a wave, and o'er it ran her bright curls,
the one o'er the other, like little wavelets.
Her eyes were as gray as a sword, and
as keen, and she had broad lids as white
as satin-flowers, and there was a fine
black ring around them, made by her
long lashes.

My lady was courted by many a fine
lord, and more than three youngsters have
I seen weep because of her coldness towards them; speeding them away out o'
the sight o' mankind (as they thought), and
casting themselves along the lush grass in

my lady's garden, there to bleat and bleat, like moon-calves for the moon.

For one lad did my heart bleed, verily. 'Twas for the young Lord of Mallow—but a lad with buttercup curls and speedwell eyes, and a smile to win the love o' any maid in her reason (though, to be sure, my lady was in her reason). He comes to me and gets between my knees, like any little eanling that might 'a' been mine own, and quoth he:

"Butter, Butter, she loves thee! Wilt thou not speak to her, and tell her that she shall be the richest lady in all England, and maid of honor to the Queen, and have more jewels than the Queen herself? Oh, Butter!" cried he.

Then said I, a-stroking of the yellow gossamer that bestrewed his shoulders, as he knelt, head bowed, between my knees, "Nay, my lord, 'tis not so that thou shalt win the Lady Margaret. She careth no more for jewels than she doth for the beads

in a rainbow; nor doth she care for riches.
And methinks a maid who would marry
just to be maid of honor to a queen would
not be an honorable maid either to herself or to her sovereign;" for so indeed
I thought.

Then saith he, "Butter, dost thou believe in love-philters?"

And I asked his meaning, for verily I
was ignorant of 't, albeit I was not ignorant in all matters. And he explained to
me that it was a drink or potion to cause
love.

Then I answered, and said, "Calamint
doth make a good brew, likewise sage,
and some flax is soothing, but methinks
none o' these would cause love."

On this he wept again, but said that I
was a good old man, and that on his return
to Mallow he would send me a gift; and so
he did—a pair o' silk hose, such as my lady
and the Queen do wear; but being mind-
ful of my station, I laid them aside for the

sake o' th' poor lad, and yesterday Marian did bring them to me, with her ten fingers through as many moth-holes. Whereupon I was minded o' th' text concerning that we lay not up treasures where moth and rust do corrupt, and at my behest Marian read me the whole of that chapter. But to return to bare facts.

It was on a certain night in March that there occurred the conversation which was the cause of this narrative. There had been news of the return of one Lord Denbeigh to Warwickshire—by report as wild a cavalier as ever fought, and a godless body to boot. Marian, who, as I have said, had always a certain knack for ghost stories and the like, froze me with her accounts o' this wild lord's doings. Quoth she:

" Fire-brace is a suiting name for him, inasmuch as 'tis a family name, and he a fire-brand to peace wheresome'er he shall go."

" Peace—peace thyself!" quoth I, hear-

ing my lady's foot along the hall. And,
o' my word, Marian had but just ceased,
and given her attention to the fire, when
in clatters my lady, with her riding-whip
stuck in her glove, and her blood-hound
Hearn in a leash. She was much wrought,
either with riding or rage, for there was a
quick red in her cheek, and she had set
her red lips until they were white. Then
took she the hound between her knees, and
plucked off her gloves. Here I did find it
my duty to speak.

"My lady," cried I, "'tis not in your mind
to baste the dog?"

"Ay, that it is," quoth she, and her lips
went tighter, and she jerked at her glove.

Then said I, "How if he leap at thy
throat?" And she answered, "Nay, he
knows better;" and with that she gripped
his collar, and let swing her whip. Then
did I bid Marian that she leave the room.
As for me, it was my duty to stay, though,
as I have given an oath to tell but the truth

2

in this narrative, I must confess that I was
in a sweat from head to foot with fear.

But the great hound crouched as though
he knew he got but what he deserved, and
when my lady had given him ten or twenty
lashes she flung wide the door, and said she,
" Get thee gone, coward !   Go fare as fares
the poor beggar thou sought'st to bite !"
and the hound slunk out.   Then turned my
mistress to me, and—"Butter," saith she,
"yon beast sought to bite an old beggar as
we came through the park, so I whipped
him.   But for naught save cruelty or dis-
obedience will I ever whip a dog ; so, Butter, the next time that thou seest me about
to lash one, keep thy counsel."   (This was
the harshest that my lady e'er spoke, either to me or to Marian.)   Then went she
to the door and called Marian.

" Come, nurse," quoth she, " I am a-weary.
Fling me some skins on the settle, and I
will lie down, and thou shalt card out my
locks with thy fingers."   So we heaped the

settle with the skins o' white bears, and thereon my lady cast herself, like a flower blown down upon a snow-bank; and by-and-by, what with the warmth and Marian's strokings, she fell into a deep sleep. But we two sate and gazed on her.

She was all clad in a tight riding-dress of green velour cloth, and her white face seemed to come from the close collar like a white lily from its sheath. She was e'er flower-like, asleep or waking, as I have said, and her pretty head was sleek and yellow, like a butterfly's wing. She was so sound that it appeared to me and Marian as though one longer breath might transform the mimicry into the actual thing—death. But by-and-by awe fell from us, as it doth ever fall, even in the presence of that which hath awed us, and my wife and I did return to our discourse concerning my Lord Denbeigh.

Quoth I to Marian, " But, wife, **may** not malice invent these tales ?"

"Nay, nay," said she, shaking her head; "as bloody a rogue as ever lived—as bloody a rogue as ever lived. They do say as how he'll set a whole tavern in a broil ere he be entered in for three minutes."

"But," quoth I, "may he not be provoked?"

"Nay, I tell thee," said she; "but he'll jump at a body's head, and cleave 't open ere a body can say 'Jesus.'"

At this I said, firmly, "I doubt not but what the poor man is most surely maligned." Whereupon Mistress Butter did wax exceeding wroth.

"Why wilt thou e'er be seeking to plead the cause o' villains?" cried she. "First that bloody beast o' my lady's, now this bloody villain o' th' devil's. I do wonder at thee, Anthony Butter." Whereat I did put in that I sometimes wondered at myself.

"For why?" quoth she.

"Why, that I ever married to be worded by a wench," said I. And at this I am most entirely sure that she would have cast her joint-stool at me, had she not been sitting on 't, and my lady's head against her knee. So she called me a "zany," and then after a little a "toad," but went on stroking my lady's hair.

And, by-and-by, back we come to his lordship.

"'Tis not alone his bloody tricks and murderous ways," quoth my wife, "that causes all Christian folk to abhor him, but he consorts with no other women than drabs and callets. Dost excuse that?"

"Nay," said I, with sufficient gravity, "then is this earl no longer a man, but a swine, and not fit for men's discussion, much less that of women."

At this reproof I saw anger again in her eye, but she was so pleased withal at having got me to call Lord Denbeigh a swine that she forebore any further personal affront.

"And yet," she went on, "they do say he

be as fine a man as a wench will walk through the rain to glimpse at, and a brave and a learned; but that he wed a Spanish maid, and she betrayed him, and so he hath vowed to hate women, one and all."

"Hast thou seen him?"

"Nay, but I've had him itemized to me by the wife o' Humfrey Lemon. A blue eye, a hooked nose, a—"

"Well, well, wife," quoth I, "if a blue eye and a hooked nose be as bad signs in a man as they be in a horse, methinks this thy villain is a very round villain."

"And so he is," affirmed she.

"Yet," said I, "there is somewhere in me a something that doth pity him."

"By my troth!" cried my wife. "I do believe, Master Butter, that thou'dst pity the Devil's wife in childbirth."

"Ay, that I would!" I made answer, with a great calmness, for I saw that she sought to rouse my spleen.

"Well, do not bellow," blurted she, "for my mistress is as sound as a gold-piece."

Then quoth my lady, a-rising up on her elbow,

"Nay, that she is not. And, moreover, she would hear all the stories concerning this bad and bloody Lord of Denbeigh!"

II.

When Marian heard my lady so speak, methought she would have swooned in verity; for she knew my lady's contempt for gossip. E'en for the first time in all her life, Marian could not find a word to her tongue.

"La! my lady," said she, and then stopped and was silent. My lady laughed at her, with her deep eyes; but as was her wont, her mouth was wondrous solemn.

"Ay, nurse," quoth she, "thou thought'st me safe i' th' Land o' Nod, but one hath ears to hear there as elsewhere." Then she reaches out one hand and plays with Marian's ruff. "Go to, nurse," says she. "Dost thou not see I am even i' th' same case with thyself? I too would gossip a little. Come, word it—word it!"

So Marian told her all that she had heard, together with a little prophesying here and there, which boded no good to my Lord Denbeigh. She told how he had e'en been a brave lad, but how in Spain he had wed with a wife who played him false; how then he had vowed vengeance on all womankind, becoming a brawler and a haunter o' taverns; how death was in his sword and lightnings in his eye.

My lady listened, and now and again she would pinch her eyelids softly with her thumb and ring-finger, as one who is deep in thought. But when Marian paused for breath, she turned to her, and quoth she,

"Nurse, thou hast often preached unto me; listen now to my preachings. Thou shalt often hear a man abused, nurse, but chiefly for that which he hath never done. This wild lord, I doubt not, hath been guilty of sorry deeds. What man hath not? But the half that thou hast told me is not to be believed."

Then went she to her room, taking Marian with her, but I saw that she was moved.

It was but the next day that my lady's uncle, Sir John Trenyon, came riding into the court. He often came in such wise, to bide for a day or two with his niece. A most courteous gentleman; red of face, blue of eye, and blithe of tongue. He had a jest for each tick o' th' clock, and a kind word for all.

"Ah, Butter," saith he, "and where is thy mistress? And thy wife, the good Dame Marian—where is she? And how about thy family? Hast thou no better prospects than of yore?"

Whereat I looked sorrowful enough, I

doubt not, for he did bid me take heart, as my first-born might have had a hare-lip or a crook-back. Then did he toss me his bridle-reins, and my lady, having heard his voice, came forth to meet him.

"So, lady-bird!" quoth he, clasping her. "I am come for no less than three reasons this time. First, to see thy bonny face. Second, to ride thy bonny Robin. Third, to inquire and seek out a certain villain of mine acquaintance, of whom you have doubtless heard;" and forthwith did he say to her of how the wicked Lord Denbeigh was the son of a friend and comrade, and of how he had known him when a lad, together with much more, at which my lady pricked up her ears, as 'twere, having all a lady's love for stories of wicked men who are not yet either old or ill-favored.

"By my troth," declared the old knight in ending, "I will take but a mouthful to stay me, and then set forth straightway in quest o' th' rascal." So having dined right heartily, he rode forth again.

Now, having related this hap to Marian, she was devoured of so great a curiosity that, as I am an honest man, I looked to see her consumed even unto her bones, as some men who burn of drink. She would have it that I must hazard a guess on the shape of Lord Denbeigh's nose, the color of his hair, and the height of his body. She forced me to wonder whether he were civil or rude of tongue. She pressed me to say whether I thought there was aye a chance of his returning with Sir John. She questioned me, in a word, until, having no answers, I was like to lose my wits, or my temper, or both together. At last comes she and sits on my knee, and tickles the back of my neck right playfully, as in the days of our wooing.

"As I live, Tony," quoth she, "we are like to have a strange story under our very noses. What if"—and here she takes my face in her two hands, and sets her chin against mine, so that I see four round blue eyes against her white brow, and am like to go blind with her thought-lessness—"what if it turns out that the Lord hath set upon our lady to be the saviour of this wicked earl?"

"Ay," cried I. "And what if the Lord hath set upon me to be the founder of a nation, like Abraham? What then?" At which she boxed my ears right sound-ly. But I could not blame her, for in the wrong I was, without doubt, although verily she had plagued me into it. So I sued for pardon, and got it, and a kiss into the bargain. But she would not leave me in peace concerning Lord Denbeigh.

When that same afternoon there comes Sir John a-riding past, and the bad earl at his side, "What dost thou say now?" quoth Marian, a-plucking me in a way that did not serve to increase good feeling betwixt

us. "Ah ha! Are not women prophet-
esses by nature?"

"Ay, by ill-nature," answered I; and for
this quip I was not forgiven for two days.

It was towards the setting of the sun
when Sir John and Lord Denbeigh rode
up to the door of Amhurste, and my lady,
knowing naught, came out at the sound of
the horses' feet, thinking only to greet her
uncle. The red light from the west shone
on her, and dabbled her white kirtle as
with blood, and her face was like one of
the red roses in her garden. So she put
up her hand to shield it, and saw the
stranger standing at her feet.

There was ne'er a nobler-looking man,
for all he might outblack Satan in his
soul: straight of body, and strong of limb,
and lofty of head. His hair was the col-
or of my lady's, and there seemed to be
ever some sunshine in it, as he moved
his head. Methought his face was fair
and goodly to look upon, albeit his lips

went downward at the corners, and there
was a droop in his broad lids. He was
clad all in a close suit of dark velvet, and
in his hand he held a black hat with a knot
of heron-plumes.

My lady stood and looked down at him
from under her long, white hand, and he
stood and looked up at my lady, as one
looks upward at a fair picture. And the
evening light crept between them. I was
ashamed of my own folly, when I did catch
myself remembering Marian's silly sayings;
but for all that, they did come back to me,
as the words of a foolish woman will return
to the wisest of men. And in truth he did
gaze up at her, as though she were more
holy than the heavens above her. And
for all her hand, the sunset found its way
unto her cheek.

What I now relate was told me by
Marian some three days after. 'Twas on
the night of the day on which Sir John
had brought the stranger to Amhurste,

and Marian was carding out my lady's tresses before her bedroom fire.

Quoth my lady, suddenly, " Nurse, didst thou see Lord Denbeigh ere he went?"

And Marian said that she had seen him.

" He hath a strange face, nurse."

" How 'strange,' my lady?"

" Why, it seems to me that each feature in it doth contradict the other. His brow is stern, and saith to his eyes, 'Ye shall not be gentle.' His eyes say to his nose, 'Spread not thy nostrils so proudly.' His nose commands his lips that they smile not; but, nurse, there was ne'er a sweeter smile on the lips o' a saint!"

Marian fell a-thinking, and pulled my lady's hair. My lady heeded it not, so Marian fell a-thinking yet more deeply.

" It is not a face that tells of a bad heart," continued my lady. " Rather it speaks of rebellion and misfortune. A sad story—a sad story."

" What is, my lady?" asked Marian; but

my lady was far away, whither Marian could not follow.

"Nurse," she saith, presently, "that were a soul worth saving." Then got she suddenly to her feet, and turned and took her nurse's hands with hers. "It shall be saved," she saith, "God helping."

And she kissed Marian, and lay down upon her bed. But Marian did tell me how that no sleep visited her lady's eyes that night. Through the darkness she could hear her turn, first on this side, then on that; then sigh and move her pillow, and sigh again.

Methought Marian would have split in sunder with importance, when Lord Denbeigh took to coming sometimes to Amhurste. 'Twas never for even an hour that he stayed; and 'twas always some question of business that brought him. But my lady and he touched hands full oft during a week, and always he would look at her with a different look from that

which his eyes did wear at other times.
And she spoke to him e'er courteously
and kindly, even as though he had been
a holy man and worthy of all reverence.

One day it chanced that my lady rode
the blue-roan out into the woods, towards
the hut of old Joan Gobble, who was crip-
pled by reason of age. My lady had me
follow her on Dumble, th' white nag, with
a pat o' butter and some wine. I was taken
up with pondering as to why my lady should
go in person to Dame Gobble's, seeing she
might have sent me alone on Dumble as
well. Be that as it may, as we rode along
by a brook-side, under the thick leaves, whom
should we come upon but my Lord Denbeigh. He was kneeling beside the water,
and holding down his hand into the brook.
As I looked I saw that his hand was be-
fouled with gore, and that the brown stream
did rush away ruddily from beneath his fingers.

My lady did not wait for me to hold

3

Robin Hood, but did swing herself from
her saddle, and was beside the earl in a
trice.   He looked up, and seeing her, did
start upon his feet.

"Nay," said she, putting out her hand,
"but tell me if I can aid thee."

And he strove to hide his hand at his
side, saying.   "'Tis but a scratch;" but
the blood ran down like water on the
grass.

"Think not to spare me the sight o'
blood," said my lady, "for I am learned in
bandaging wounds."   And certes she was,
seeing that every soul at Amhurste did
come to her for healing, let a cat but
scratch them.   And she took his hand between her two fair hands (having drawn off
her gloves), and saw that his wrist was deeply severed as with a knife.   But she asked
him no questions, telling him only to stoop
while she cleansed his hand sufficiently to
bind it.   And as she laid it in the water,
and pressed the lips of the wound together,

he said unto her in a low tone, not meaning that I should hear him,

"Would that thou couldst wash my soul
as thou hast washed my hand!"

She looked straight into his eyes, with
her own so clear and honest, like a dog's
(meaning no disrespect to my lady, as God
knows), and she answered him and saith,

"It were well worth the washing, my lord;
but an higher than I must cleanse it."

And he saith, "There is none higher."

At that my lady's blood rose in her
cheek, but she besought him that he would
not speak to her in such wise. When
she had made a compress of the napkins
in the basket wherein I was carrying
Dame Gobble's butter, and had stanch-
ed the blood, she unwound the ribbon
from her silver hunting-horn, and cast it
about his neck for a rest to his wounded arm. Then he did bend down his
head and kissed the ribbon, and my lady
turned quickly, and got upon the roan,

and rode away at so smart a pace that methinks Dame Gobble's butter and wine did reach her in a closer conjunction than she could have found pleasant.

When I told Marian of this encounter, merely by the way of a bit of gossip, she did smile in such a wise that I was minded to cuff a woman for the first time in a long life.

It was that same night that Marian did tell me how that she feared the earl was in danger of some sort, judging by certain words that my lady had let fall in her sleep. I noticed how that my lady seemed restless, and would start at the clap o' a door, or when Herne did come suddenly upon her. And one day she leaned from a window, as I swept up the rose-leaves from the grass on the east terrace, and called to me to come thither. She was as white as her kirtle, and her gray eyes were dark like water before a storm. She did not look at me, but beyond into the air.

So I waited, having plucked off my cap, and my lady stood looking, looking; and after a while she saith,

"Thou hast aye been a true and faithful servant unto me : therefore I am about to give unto thee a great charge."

And I said, "My lady, thou knowest that thou canst trust me;" and in truth I could say no more, for my throat was stiff.

And she continued and said,

"Thou must be to-night at the Red Deer, and that by nine of the clock. One will be there in whom we have both deep interest. I cannot tell thee more. Take thy sword with thee, but have no fear— thou wilt have no cause to use it. Yet, lest thou be fearful, take it with thee." And she said, "Thou wilt remember?"

"My lady, when have I e'er forgotten word of thine?" Whereat she did put out her fair hand to me, saying, "Never," and there were tears in her eyes.

So that night (for the first time in many

years) did I find myself within the doors
of the Red Deer.　A cosey place it was,
despite the wine-bibbers that did profane it;
and the inn-keeper's wife, a most buxom,
eye-pleasing wench, with three sturdy boys
aye clambering about her.　As I looked,
some hard and sinful thoughts did visit
my heart concerning the bounty that the
Lord had lavished upon one who was a
barterer of wine, when I, who had lived
ever a temperate and (in so far as was in
my power) a godly life, should remain child-
less.　But I did conquer at last, bidding
Satan get behind me, and was left in peace
to toast my feet, and to ponder as to who
it was that my lady had sent me thither to
mark.　Had I not loved my lady with all
my heart, methinks I could not have stood
the terms that were heaped upon me by
the brawlers.　I will not repeat the foul
slanders; suffice it to say, I sustained for
one half hour what few men are called
upon to endure throughout a lifetime.

At last, the newness being gone, they left me in peace, and I, being settled safely in my corner, did set to work to watch the door.

Who should enter at that very moment but my Lord Denbeigh! He was wrapped in a long brown cloak, and wore a broad hat, unornamented by plume or buckle, pulled down over his eyes. He came and tossed himself into a chair near the fire, and sat there pondering upon the coals, with his legs out in front of him. Now, I have ever had a woman-weakness for a goodly leg in man, and the splendid limbs of Lord Denbeigh did witch me into a steadier gaze than that which civility doth permit. This by-and-by he did notice, and so spoke to me.

"At what art thou staring, ancient?" quoth he, not unkindly. So I told him, whereupon he laughed somewhat.

"Methinks thou art but a doting body," he said, "and yet is thy face familiar.

What now?   Hast thou e'er met with me before?"

Then did I lie right roundly, being, to confess the truth, not a little afraid.

"Out on thee," saith his lordship; "the truth is not in thee.   I ne'er forget a face; how, then, shall I forget a face such as ' thine?   Certes I have seen thee before. Wilt thou colt me?"

And again lied I — blackly, most abominably.

"As thou wilt," quoth he; "but thy face is known to me, for all that."

It was at this time that the door opened again, and there did enter a stripling, clad all in dark maroon velvet, wrapped also about with a long cloak, and having a velvet bonnet pulled down over his brows i' th' manner o' Lord Denbeigh's.   One could see naught o' his visage for the shadow from his head-gear.   The revelers scarce noted his entrance, being far gone in drink, and some having departed, and others asleep.

The lad came and stood near the fire, and
I saw that he looked at Lord Denbeigh
from under his drooping bonnet—the earl
having withdrawn unto a table apart, with
a glass of wine and some papers, and his
sword across the table. Even as I looked
the boy turned, and went over, and leaned
on the table to finger the heavy sword. My
heart was afraid within me, for there was a
dark light in the eyes that flashed up at the
youth from under Lord Denbeigh's stern
brows. I was nigh unto them, being but a
stride or two apart, and so marked all that
passed between them.

" By my troth," quoth his lordship, " a valiant crack !"

" Meaning me ?" quoth the lad, smiling.

"Ay, meaning thee, Sir Insolence. Dost
thou know how to handle thine own sword,
that thou handlest a stranger's so freely ?"

"Even so. But I meant not to vex thee.
In truth, I am come to thee on an errand
of life and death ;" and as he spoke, he did

doff his bonnet and toss it upon the table, and the firelight and candlelight did leap upon his fair curls, and as I saw his face it was the face of my lady. The earl did start half-way to his feet, and his face was first like fire and then like snow.

"Margaret!" he saith, back of his teeth, as 'twere.

And the lad smiled, leaning still upon the table.

"Nay; my sister is called so," he said, "but my name is Robert, and I am the Lord of Amhurste and her brother. Haply she hath mentioned me unto your lordship."

The earl stared as one who sees a ghost (though I believe not in them myself), and he saith, "Whence comest thou? All think that thou art dead."

And the boy said,

"Nay, but I would not that any besides thee knew of my whereabouts. As to thee, I know more concerning thee even than my sister, and it is for her sake that I come to thee to-night."

And my lord saith, " For her sake ?"

" Even so. I am come to persuade thee that thou wilt not go on the errand thou wottest of two nights hence. There are those who do mean thee death. It is certain that thy life is plotted against. Surely thou wilt be warned?" And as I looked, the color left the lad's face, and he grew white as any woman. Almost I could have sworn it was my lady's face. Line for line, eyelash for eyelash, look for look. And methought no mother's heart e'er yearned towards her new-born babe as yearned my heart towards the youth. It seemed as though I must cry out to him. To see him thus after five weary years; to be so near him, and yet unable to touch even the latchet of his shoes, or to hear his voice calling my name. I trembled and was blind with longing. When at last I did look up, he said again, " Surely, thou wilt be advised ?"

The earl leaned with his forehead set in his clasped hands, and by-and-by he said,

" It is impossible. Would that I could !"

And the lad said,

" Nay, it is not impossible. Thou canst save thine own life with a word."

And Lord Denbeigh answered him :

" My life is not worth even a word," and he did not lift up his forehead from his hands.

Then said my master, " Thy life may be worth less than naught to thee, but to others its price is above their own." And again he was as pale as any girl.

And he spoke again and said, " Thou wilt not go ? Thou wilt be warned ?"

And again did the man answer, saying, " Impossible."

Then saith my master,

" Lord Denbeigh, if thou goest to London on the morrow, I will follow thee there.

Nay, thou canst not prevent me. And think you my sister's heart will be warmer towards thee if her brother's blood be spilled at thy behest?"

And the earl sat with his stern eyes on the lad, and he said,

" Thy blood will ne'er be spent at my behest. I do forbid thee to follow me."

And the lad said,

"I am not to be forbidden." So they stood and looked at one another. And all at once the boy put out his hand ('twas my lady's very gesture) and took the earl's sleeve, and saith he in a gentle voice,

" Thou wert a man after God's own heart did not thou let Satan consort with thee."

Then turned Lord Denbeigh with a laugh that was not merry. And he saith,

"As thou quotest Scripture to me, select thy texts with greater care. Even to my mind there doth come one more suiting; for even as Job, ' I am a brother to dragons, and a companion to owls.' "

Then saith the lad, still with his hand
on the man's arm,

" Is it not the more to thy discredit that
thou, who couldst be brother to Christ, do
make brothers of dragons?   Verily, my
lord, I am bold through my sister, for methinks it is thus that she would have answered thee."

And the man turned away as though to
hide his face.

III.

Lord Robert spoke with Lord Denbeigh at some length, but he was not to be
turned from his purpose (which, methought,
must be a very strange and grewsome one,
judging by their words).   So finally they
went out separately, and I got me back to
Amhurste.

The next morning I did relate to my
lady all that had passed, but mentioning no
names, as I saw that she wished it not.

And when I was finished she bade me go straightway to London and find out the whereabouts of Lord Denbeigh. Moreover, she told me that she herself would be there shortly with Marian, and that they two would lodge at the house of Marian's aunt, one Mistress Pepper, a linen-draper's wife. At this I wondered greatly, the more that she should keep silent concerning her brother than that she should follow him to London. And all that I could think was that Lord Robert was in some dire conspiracy, likewise the earl, and that she feared for the lives of one or both. So we all go to London, I earlier than my lady and Marian.

For a day I lost sight of Lord Denbeigh (whom I had followed closely all the way from Warwickshire), but the next afternoon I marked him as he passed along a by-way, and heard him speak with some one of his friends, naming a tavern where he would meet him at a certain hour that night.

So first I found out where the tavern was, then straight to my lady and acquainted her with all that I had discovered.

She said naught but to commend my diligence, and she went whiter than a just washed sheep at shearing-time. Quoth I to myself, "Butter, there is more here than thou wottest of;" which was very true.

That night, a little before the hour set upon, I did get me to the tavern, and lurked quietly in the shadows where none might observe; and there, verily, was the earl and him with whom he had spoken in the afternoon. He had but said a word or so when Lord Robert entered, and went and stood at his elbow, but did not touch him or pluck at his cloak. Albeit, the earl seemed to feel his presence, for shortly he turned and saw the lad.

"How!" quoth he. "Thou here?"

And the boy said, "I told thee I would follow thee."

And Lord Denbeigh answered him,

" Dost thou know of what thou speak‧
est ?",

And the lad said, " Verily I know, and
thou mayest trust me;" and with that he
muttered two or three words under his
breath, which, because of mine old ears, I
could not catch. And the two men started
and looked at one another. Then the earl
did turn to his friend, saying to him that
they could indeed trust the lad. So they
three clasped hands. When that was done,
Lord Denbeigh turns to my master, and
saith he, " Hast thou thy dirk with thee?"
and the lad answered that he had both
sword and dagger.

" Not that there is any danger," quoth
the earl, " but that thou mayest feel easy."

But the lad said, " There is danger, as I
have told thee; and thou art putting thy
life in jeopardy." At this Lord Denbeigh
only laughed; but as they went out into the
street I marked that he kept the lad close at
his side, almost as a mother keeps a child.

4

The night was still and cold, and the sky full of little white clouds that lapped the one over the other, like shells on a sea-shore. Now and again the moon would strike through, in a long, bright ray, that seemed like a keen blade or lance severing the misty air. The three went on and on, through many winding ways, and still I followed, for I knew not into what danger the lad might be hastening.

All at once, in a dark turning, there came the clang of swords and a rushing and scuffling, but no cry of any kind; and methought the silence was more hideous than sound. Stiff as were my old joints with disuse, I drew my sword and lay about me lustily, striving to get between the villains and my young master (which is no credit to me, as I was so wrought with rage that I verily believe I would have no more felt the thrust of a rapier than Marian's housewife the prick of a needle). But there was no method in

aught, neither could anything be seen; for
the moon had withdrawn behind the clouds,
and we seemed to be fighting underneath
clear water, so pale and ghastly was the
light shed about us from the pale clouds.
And as I struck out with my sword I saw
a fellow in a mask close with Lord Denbeigh, lifting a dagger high in his hand,
while another rascal pinned the earl's hands
to his sides. And even as I looked, the lad
leaped between, and the thin knife went
deep into his breast. At the same time
there was a louder clash of swords, and
a thudding of men's bodies together, and
the masked wretches turned about and did
take to their heels with a good will. So
I sheathed my sword and ran forward.

Lord Denbeigh and his friend were bending over the lad, who lay out-stretched between them, with his white face turned up
to the white sky, looking like the face of
a dead man at the bottom of a clear pool.
Then could I not withhold my grief, but

cried aloud, "My master, my master!" and
tried to feel with my trembling old hands
for the wound.

Then said the earl, "Not here! I will
carry him to a place of safety." And he
lifted the boy in his arms, as though he
had been a hurt child.

When the other saw that, he laid hold
on Lord Denbeigh's arm, saying, "What
mean you? are you distraught? There is
but scarce time by the clock."

And the earl said, "Go you on. I must
take this boy where his wound can be
bound."

"Nay," said the man. "I tell you, you
are mad!"

And Lord Denbeigh turned on him, and
spoke in a harsh voice:

"I have said I will not go. I have done
with thee and thine. Go thy ways ere it
be too late;" and he passed on and left the
man to swallow the moonshine with his
great gaping mouth.

And he saith unto me, "Follow closely."
So by-and-by we came to a great gray
house, and Lord Denbeigh opened the door
and bade me enter with him.

We passed through a vast hall, and up a
ponderous staircase, and into a room. A
fire was burning on the hearth, and there
was a fantastic kind of lamp swinging from
a silver chain above the bed's foot.

I guessed rightly that this was his lordship's own apartment. He laid the lad on
the bed, and fell to undoing his doublet of
black velvet. I did see him set to shiver-
ing, as 'twere, when he noted the red stains
on the shirt underneath, and my heart
stood still within me. Then he opened
the red linen, and did put in his hand gently to feel if the heart were yet beating;
but no sooner had he done this than he
gave a strange cry, and drew out his hand
dripping with blood, and stood staring and
trembling. At the same moment the lad
stirred, and opened his eyes, and began to

clutch feebly at his doublet, drawing it together. I made naught of it until Lord
Denbeigh did turn to me, with the face of
a dead man, and quoth he, " Stay here while
I fetch women," and so rushed out like one
in truth distraught.

Then did it all come upon me, and I
knew that the face upon which I looked
was the face of my lady.

Ere another second had passed I heard
the earl's voice without, and he spoke with
a woman:

" Do thou go instantly and clothe the
lady within in some of thy garments; and
have care that thou say no word to any of
what hath happened, else will it not be
well for thee."

When I heard the tone in which he
spoke, methought in truth it would not be
well for her did she not heed his commands.

Shortly there entered a woman most
marvellous fair, with hair that seemed spun

of black taffetas, and a skin like a white jasmine. When she saw the blood her lips whitened, and she did close them more closely, but no cry escaped her. Where-at I was much ashamed, remembering the hullabaloo that I had raised.

I turned aside while she disrobed my lady and clothed her in clean linen, and drew down the sheets, placing her between them. But the blood still flowed in spite of all bandages, and the fair linen was soon crimson.

And when all was prepared, the woman went to the door and said, "You can enter," and the earl came into the chamber again. When, however, he did see my lady he cried out, "God in heaven! she will bleed to death!" and he called the woman, and showed her how to stanch the wound. Then, when the steps of the surgeon were heard in the hall without, he said unto her, "Remember. She is thy sister, and thieves have stabbed her for the jewels

on her neck." And she answered him, "I
will remember."

And all this time methought I was in
an evil dream, and that Marian, for some
spite, would not awaken me.

How it came about, to this day I recol-
lect not, but ere two weeks had sped we
were again at Amhurste, and my lady in
her own bower, under Marian's care. As
to that, Marian had been with my lady
ever since the fatal night whereon she was
nigh done to death by that masked ruffian.

The earl did go himself to fetch her
from Mistress Pepper's, and after that she
came neither of us saw the sloe-eyed
woman any more.

None had known of my lady's stay in
town, saving my lady herself, Lord Denbeigh, the black-eyed woman (who never
uttered word more, good or bad, after that
she had said, " I will remember "), Marian,
and me. So besides us five no one was
the wiser.

It was towards the last of May that my lady did beg that we would lift her out to sit in a long-chair on the east terrace. The birds were at their morning gossiping in the shrubbery, and the air was most sweet with the breath of the white lilacs. My lady looked like a snow-wreath fallen suddenly among the greenery of spring, but her eyes did peep softly, like bluebells, from the snows of her face. Methought she was all white and blue, like the heavens above her, and her hair made sunshine over all. Herne, the blood-hound, lay at her feet, and would not be stirred, though for sport my lady had Marian to tempt him with some comfits.

While we were all there, and my lady showing us how the light shined through her thin hands, and discoursing right merrily, there came a page and handed her a letter. Back fell she among her pillows, and her eyelids dropped over her eyes, like snow-flakes fallen on violets. Anon she opened the letter, and having read it, said unto Marian, "Nurse, go bid him hither." So Marian beckoned me, and we left her. As we entered the house, who should pass us but my Lord of Denbeigh, and o' my word he was whiter than my lady, if anything, and wrapped as usual in a long cloak. He seemed not to see us, and we went on in silence.

Here transpires the only part of this narrative concerning which I am reluctant to write. I will out with it, however, and the Almighty knows that I have not done with repentance even yet. So be it. There was a window overhanging the terrace where my lady sat (the window out of which she had leaned to speak to me about repairing to the Red Deer). But let me not defer longer. I, Anthony Butter, of respectable parents, and counted among my fellows and betters an honest man, did go to this window, and did most deliberately listen to the words that passed between my mistress and the Earl of Denbeigh. In fact (for I have sworn to keep back no jot or tittle of the truth), I did speed me so fast that I was at the window ere his lordship reached my lady's side.

He came slowly, but his look went before him, and was fast upon my lady's face ere he himself was within ten yards of her. When at last he was come to her side, he did stand and look down on her, but uttered no word. And also my lady did look down, and there was a light like sunset on her cheek.

Then suddenly did he drop upon his knees beside her, and bowed down his head upon her knee and was silent. Then my lady (God forever keep her!) did turn her eyes quickly, and stole a look to see that no one was nigh (God forgive my dastardly presence!), and did reach out one pale hand, half fearfully as 'twere, and did let it rest upon the man's bowed head, as a white rose-leaf falls and rests on the

earth.   And she said but two words, " My
friend;" yet methought all love was in
them.   Whereat he raised his head and
looked at her, and it is so that men look
upward when they pray.   He took her
hands with his and held them to his breast,
and he saith, " Dear saint, if thou forgivest
me, wilt thou but kiss my brow?"   And
she bended forward and kissed him; and
he trembled, calling her by name; and she
asked him what he would with her.   Then
kneeling at her side, he spoke to her, and
his words were as follows:

" Thou hast heard of my life and of my
misfortunes, but all hath not been told
thee.   Grant me but patience for a moment, that I myself may tell thee all."

And she saith unto him, " Say on."

So he spoke and said, " There is much
that I may not tell thee, yet part I will tell
thee, for that I must.   Thou hast heard
how that my wife—" But he could not
continue, so dropped his face into my

lady's hands, and she waited for him, saying softly,

"I will understand what thou dost not
say. Be not troubled, but speak out thy
soul to me;" and presently he told her
more. As I do live, never listened I to
sadder story. So piteous it was that my
tears fell down like rain, and I was sore
afraid that my sighing would discover my
whereabouts. But the Almighty is mer-
ciful even to sinners, and I remained un-
noted. 'Twas the old tale of love and
treachery; a false wife and a friend who
was a villain.

The earl had killed the man (but in fair
encounter), and his wife he had brought
back, never to be as husband to her more,
but to preserve her from further sin. And
I do maintain that 'twas a noble act, and
I did quite forgive him the blood of his
betrayer. Methought my lady did forgive
him too, for she did but stroke his hair
softly, saying ever and anon, " Poor soul !"

or "God help thee!" And by-and-by he lifted his face, and saith, "But the worst is yet to tell thee."

And she said again, "Say on."

And he trembled again, but spoke out bravely: "My wife yet lives. It was she who bound thy wounds."

Now at this I thought to see my lady swoon; but she only smiled, though better had one seen her weep than smile in such wise. And she saith, "I have known that these many days;" and she leaned towards him, and placed both hands upon his head, saying, "Weep not. I hold thee guiltless. Do not weep."

But he sobbed, clasping her knees, as one whose heart is broken, saying now and again below his breath, "O God! O God!"

If there be this side the stars a more awful sight than the sight of a strong man in tears, God grant I may ne'er behold it, for surely I should die of pity. Doth it please God that I resemble Abraham in the matter of age, if in none other, ne'er will that scene fade from my memory—my lady, so wan and white and narrow, like a tall lily over which a rude wind hath swept, and at her knee the strong man, bowed as a little lad that saith his prayers, clasping her kirtle and her hands, as though one sinking in deep waters were to grasp at a floating stem of flowers for support. And after a while, when the violence of his grief was spent, he saith unto her,

"I sail for Spain with Essex on the morrow, as thou knowest; but it doth remain for me to tell thee why I go. It is for that I think the lad, thy brother, hath been a prisoner of war these many years, and I go to bring him to thee."

And she sat and looked at him as though her heart had leaped from her breast into his body; but she spake no words save only, "God keep thee; God go with thee."

And suddenly he saith unto her, as though the words would forth,

"I loved thee from the moment that I saw thee. Let me but tell thee that."

She whispered, saying, "It was even so with me." And he lifted his eyes and looked at her. Then fled I, as though I had drawn away the veil from the sanctuary, for I thought that God would surely smite me for having beheld that look.

So Lord Denbeigh sailed with the Earl of Essex for the war in Spain, and my lady's soul left her body and went with him; for surely 'twas but her body that remained at Amhurste. All day long would she sit silent, nor move, nor look, and her hands the one upon the other before her, as who should say, "I am done with all things, whether of work or of play." So passed the months, and ever and anon some report would reach the village of the wild earl's deeds in Spain, and

of how he would fight ten men with one
arm wounded and the blood in his eyes,
and such like tales.   But no word came
direct, either through letters or friends.
So passed the months, and it was nigh to
August, and the fighting was over for the
time, when one day, with a clattering as
of a horsed army, there comes dashing into
the court two cavaliers on horseback, and
one of them was my Lord of Denbeigh.
Ere I could look at the other he had leaped to the ground, and had me about the
neck a - kissing me as roundly as ever a
wench in the market-place.   And lo! when
I looked, it was Lord Robert in very truth.
He was grown out of all knowledge, and
as brown as a nut, but as big and as bonny a lad as ever clapped hand to sword.

When I could turn my eyes from him
upon the earl, I saw that he was waxed
as pale as death, and wore his arm in a
kerchief, and that there was a great red
streak adown his temple, clean through his

5

right eyebrow. And his splendid flanks and chest were hollow, like those of a good steed that lacketh fodder. But when he stood and leaned against his horse's neck and smiled at us, methought he was by far the goodliest man that ever I had looked upon. His teeth were as white as the foam on his horse's bit, and there was a deep nick at the corner of his mouth, like that at the mouth of a girl.

Then must I call Marian, and send her to break the news to my lady. So in a moment she comes rushing down along the stair-way, like a branch that is blown suddenly from the top o' a tall tree, and so into Lord Robert's arms; and he catches her to his heart, and so stands holding her; and they make no motion nor any sound whatever. Then turns the earl away, and leaves them together. But I marked that his eyes were brimming, and that there was a quiver in his lip.

Ere night all is known to us: how Lord

Robert had been a prisoner in Spain all these years, yet was he treated with courtesy at the behest o' some wench. But he did not love her, God be praised! And 'tis in my mind to this day how he might have wed her, and how the earl did relate to him his bitter experiences with a Spanish wife. Ay, that is my firm opinion. All this and more did we hear, laughing and weeping by turns. But it was not until Lord Robert saw my lady alone that she heard of how the earl had saved him at the risk of his own life, all but bearing him in his arms through the enemy, hewing his way right and left. And, moreover, Lord Robert did tell how that the blood from that cut on the earl's temple did in truth run down into his eyes and blind him, but how that he dashed it back and slew the man who wounded him, and so they escaped.

The next morning, as I did sally forth with my cross-bow to have a shot at a

screech - owl which for some nights past
had disturbed Marian's slumbers, she in
her turn having disturbed mine, I did see
Lord Denbeigh come out upon the terrace
and throw himself down along the grass,
beneath a tulip-tree, with a book. But he
read not, lying very quiet, with his head
raised up upon one hand and his elbow
sunk in the soft turf.   And as the sunlight struck through the leaves upon his
glittering hair, and his face like marble,
I could not but pause to gaze on him, so
noble looked he.   But his eyes were far
away, and his thoughts with them.

It was for this that he did not hear my
lady coming until she stood beside him,
and her white gown brushed his cheek.
But seeing her, he leaped to his feet, and
the blood ran along his face, and then seemed all to settle in the long wound, leaving
him more pale than before.   And she said
to him,

"Nay, do not rise, for thou art weak yet;"

but he would not be seated, so they stood there, side by side in the fair morning light. And presently she puts out her hand (no one ere reached out their hand as did my lady), and she just lays it on his sleeve, and saith she, " I am come to thank you — to thank you with all my heart and soul—" and there a sob chokes her, and she can say no more.

Again the blood swept up across his brow; and he said, " For God's love, say no more."

But she answered, saying, " Nay, I have so much to say." And she came nearer to him for a little space; and her head drooped downward, like a flower full of rain. And she did knit and unknit her white fingers as they hung before her. And she saith, " There is no guerdon worthy such a knight, but if an thou—"

Then all on a sudden did she reach out both arms towards him, and her fair hands, palms upward, and the scarlet leaped to her very brow; but she lifted her little head proudly, albeit her eyes were dropped downward, and she said unto him, " Take me, for I am thine."

And he trembled from head to foot, and parting his lips as though to speak, reached out his arms and clasped her.

And when I realized what I had done, I did drop my cross-bow and took to my heels, like one followed by goblins.

Now, even as I hope to be saved, I but just come to recognize that this was my second eavesdropping. So be it. I have vowed, and must keep my vow.

It was all made clear to me that night, when Marian did relate to me how that the Spanish woman had slain herself by swallowing flame. At which (though mightily pleased, God forgive me, on account of my lady and the earl) I was more than ever thankful that Lord Robert had escaped alive and unwed out o' th' clutches o' th' Spanish wench. And here it occurreth to me that I have not yet told that Marian did know from the first of my lady's going up to town dressed as her brother. This I record more on account of its being a marvellous instance of a woman's keeping her tongue than to shame Marian, who hath often read how that wives should submit themselves unto their husbands as unto the Lord. Howbeit, all ended so happily that I had not the heart to scold her.

With the first frosts of October my lady and the earl were wed. Methought the queen herself could not have had a finer wedding, and certes no woman could have had a nobler spouse. He was yet pale from his wounds, but most soldierly of bearing and proud of carriage. He was clad all in white, like my lady. A more beauteous apparel I have never seen.

His doublet was of cloth of silver, with a close jerkin of white satin embroidered in silver and little pearls. His girdle and the scabbard of his sword were of cloth of

silver, with golden buckles.   His poniard
and sword were hilted and mounted in
gold, together with many blazing orders
and richer devices that I know not how
to enumerate.

My lady's gown was all of white satin,
sewn down the front with little pearls, like
those on my lord's jerkin, and her ruff was
of soft lace, not stiff, as was the fashion,
but falling about her bosom most modestly
and becomingly.   Lord Robert, methinks,
was eke as goodly, after his way, as either
his sister or Lord Denbeigh, being close
clad from head to foot in crimson sarcenet,
slashed all with cloth of gold.   My lady had
given me some suiting clothes for the occasion; and as for Marian, methought in her
new gown of sea - green taffeta, with her
new ruff and head-gear, that she looked as
fair a matron as any mother of fine lads in
all England.

IV.

Seven months they had been wed, and it was May again.   Methought such love had never been on earth since Eden.   'Twas gladness but to see them.   And all, more-o'er, was so well with Lord Robert, who, folks did say, was in mighty great favor at court, and like to become a shining light in the land.

'Twas on a May morning.   The trees were a-lilt with birds, and the sound of waters set all the winds a-singing.   All at once comes my lord, and sets his hand on my shoulder.   Then know I that some-thing dire hath happened.   And he saith, " Friend, where is thy mistress ?"

And I tell him that she is out among her roses.

Then saith he all at once, " The Queen hath sent for me—I must to war."

And I could do naught but stare at him.
And he said to me: "In an hour I must
be gone. Say naught to thy mistress. I
will go don a suiting dress, and do thou
bring me my sword and give it into my
hand."

And he went, returning shortly, and I
gave him the sword. It was then that we
heard the voice of my lady without, and
she sang a song of the spring-tide. The
words I have ne'er forgot, though I did
but hear them once:

"For O! For O!
The cowslips blow,
And the ground's all gold below me;
The speedwell's eye
Peers up so bli'
I swear it seems to know me!

" The lady-smocks
In silver frocks
Do flout the sonsy clover;
The humble bee
Consorts wi' me
And hails me for a rover.

"Then trip, then trip,
  And if ye slip
    Your lad will lend a hand O ;
  The lass in green
  With black, black een,
    Is the fairest in the land O."

And as the earl listened methought he would have fallen, grasping my shoulder, old man as I was, and bending down his head upon it. And I did stay him with my arm, as though he had been my very son — for old age is father to all men.

So my lady comes in, with her gold hair blowing, and her white kirtle full of red roses, and seeing her lord goes to meet him. But when she noted the soldierly fashioning of his dress, and the sword girt at his thigh, she opened her lips as though to cry out, but no sound escaped them. And her kirtle slipped from her hold, and the red roses lay between them like a pool of blood.

Then she saith unto him, "Tell me. Quick, quick!"

And he lifts her to him, and saith, "Sweetheart, my Queen hath bidden me come fight for her and for my country."

And she saith naught, only clasps him.

But by-and-by she cries out, saying, "Go not! Go not! Else wilt thou kill me." And so speaking, falls like one dead at her lord's feet.

Then I, running like one distraught to fetch Marian, do tilt pell-mell into Lord Robert, who hath come down to Amhurste for a week or so of rest.

"Heydey!" quoth he. "What Jack-a-lent hath frighted thee?" And I told him all. Never a word said he, but went straight-way and got upon his horse, and clapped spurs to its sides, and so out of sight.

And all that night my lady lay nigh to death, so that there was ne'er a thought in the breast of any for another soul. There-fore Lord Robert was not missed.

Ere two days were past came a man with despatches, and we found out how that Lord Robert had substituted himself for the earl (having acquainted the Queen with the circumstances—and he being, moreover, so great a favorite), and how the Queen had granted Lord Denbeigh leave to remain in England a while longer.

And so his lordship was with his lady when their child was born, but Lord Robert was killed in the wars.

They grieved sore for him, and for many weeks would not be comforted. And even it was said that the Queen mourned for him, and did banish all festivities from court for the space of several days.

But like as the stars do pale in the morning sky, so pales the orb of sorrow before the rays of the great sun, happiness.

And though he was ne'er forgotten, and though the tears would spring to my lady's eyes heard she but his name mentioned, yet she did smile again and was happy.

It chanced but this morning that Marian
and I, leaning from the window that over-
looks the east terrace, did see a most winsome sight.

'Twas a fair morning, and May again,
and on such mornings as these my lady
would go forth on the east terrace with the
child.   And there grow all such sweet flowers as my lady loves—the red mule-pinks,
and dame's-violets, such as are sweet o' even-
ings, but marvellous fair to look upon both
by sunlight and moonlight.   And the south
wall was all thick with the yellow violets, so
that my lady's head looked like the head
o' a saint against a golden platter.   And
there did my lady sit, on a quaintly
wrought bench, with the little lord.

And this morning, when she was seated,
and the babe curled against her bosom, and
Marian and myself thinking o' the pictures
o' the Virgin Mary and the blessed Jesus
(saving that my lady's kirtle was all of
white and gold, like the lilies, knotted in

her waistband), she looked up on a sudden, and lo! there was the master coming along over the grass towards her. When he saw who it was that sat there, he doffed his plumed hat like as though it had been the Virgin Mary for very truth, and he paused a minute, but then came on.

When my lady saw him who he was, there came a fair red o'er all the white o' her throat and face; ay, and withal over her very bosom. And she put up one white hand, with her wedding-ring on't, and made as though she would shield the sun from the babe's eyes.

And all this time my lord came slowly over the grass, as though the sweet sight did pleasure him both far and near. And when he was approached, he stood, still with his hat in his hand, and looked down at the babe and its mother, and was silent.

Then the child, feeling mayhap that its father was near, twisted over towards him, reaching out its waxen arm, and smiled right knowingly; whereat my lord did pluck the great plume out o' his hat and lay it across my lady's bosom; moreover, he knelt and put an hand on the babe, but his arm he held about his wife.

Then did she draw both my lord and the child to her, and pressed them against her, but her face she lifted Godwards.

And something spoke within our hearts that we turned and left the window.

THE FARRIER LASS O' PIPING PEBWORTH.

HUMFREY LEMON, meeting Bered Turnip, before the "Red Deer," doth speak as follows:

Whom have we here? Well, well, by my troth! 'tis none other than Bered Turnip, the farrier, as I do live! Come for an alms-drink, comrade. Would I had as many gold-pieces as we have burnt al-nights i' this very tavern! And is it thus we meet after all these years? It doth seem but yesterday that we supped under this very roof as juvenals. Dost thou mind thee o' the night that we gave old Gammer Lick-the-Dish a bath in his own

6

sack, for that he served us in a foul jerkin?
By'r lay'kin, those were days! Well, well,
to meet thee thus! Though, believe it or
not, as thou wilt, I had such a pricking i'
my thumbs but an hour gone that I was of
a mind to roar you like any babe with a
pin in his swaddling-bands. Thou wast
my beau-peer i' those times; and we are
kin by profession, moreover. How be Mistress Turnip and thy eight lads? Ha!
ha! Dost remember how old Anthony
Butter—him who was gardener at Amhurste Castle, ye mind—dost thou remember in what spite he held thee because o'
those eight little salads o' thine? A always said a married with an eye to a's
posterity; and o' my word a's been cock-
eyed e'er since, for's posterity has e'er kept
him on the lookout: never chick or child
hath Mistress Butter given him.

Quoth he to me one day, a-setting of
's chin in 's thumb and forefinger (thou
mind'st his solemn ways)—quoth he to me,

"Lemon," quoth he, "would I knew why the Lord doth seem to look with a more bounteous favor on such as are farriers, than on such as be followers of other trades; for methinks, what with thee, and Turnip, and Job Long-pate, who bides in Dancing Marston, England will owe the chief o' her future population to black-smiths." I quoth, to humor him, quoth I, "Belike, Master Butter," quoth I, "the Almighty hath gotten wisdom by experience, and doth purpose to put no further trust in gardeners." Whereat he waxed so wrathful, that for the sake o' my breeches I took to my heels. But, Lord! it doth seem as though a had a spite against th' very children o' others. Thou mindest my Keren? By'r lay'kin, 'twill not stick i' my old pate how that thou hast not been in these parts since my Keren could 'a' walked under a blackberry-bramble without so much as tousling her tresses. Well, a grew up a likely lass, I can tell thee!

Sure thou mindest why we—my wife and I—did come to call her Keren? Go to! Thou dost! 'Tis the jest o' th' place to this day. Well, then, if thou dost not, I'll be at the pains o' telling thee; for methinks 'twas a wise thought. We did christen her Keren-Happuch; "for," quoth my wife, "when that we be pleased with her, we can call her Keren—which is as sweet-sounding a name as a maid can have; and, on the other hand, when we be wroth with her, we can call her Happuch—which sure would be a rough name even for thy trotting mare Bellibone." Ha! ha! And thereby, comrade, hangs another tale, as Master Shakespeare was wont to say. My wife, thou must know, hath e'er been a loyal admirer o' our gracious Queen, and it comes to her ears one day as how her Majesty did ride a-horseback most excellent well. Naught would do but that I must let Mistress Lemon mount for a ride upon my gray mare Bellibone. Now Bellibone, though as willing a nag as ever ambled, did think far more o' getting to her journey's end than o' the manner in which she did accomplish the journey; and, I will say, a trotted as though a was for breaking th' stones on th' Queen's highway, instead o' getting o'er 'em. Well, I did what I could to dissuade Mistress Lemon from her enterprise, but a was as firm as one o' my surest driven nails in a new shoe. So a let her go. Couldst thou but 'a' seen her when she was returned an hour after! Ha! ha! ha! a was for breaking my head with my own pincers.

"Dost thou call that devil's-riding-horse 'Bellibone?'" quoth she, with what breath there was left to her. "By my troth, I think she hath not another bone in her whole body besides her backbone!"

But I spake o' Keren. Thou knowest that even as a lass she had a sharp tongue o' her own—as keen as a holly leaf, by my troth. So be it. 'Twas one day nigh unto

Martlemas that old Butter did undertake to chide her for conducting herself after the manner o' a lad rather than o' a lass.

Quoth she to him, a-setting of her little black pate to one side, and of her little brown arms akimbo—quoth she, " Since the Lord hath not made me a lad," quoth she, " I cannot more than act like one; and so I will do !"

Quoth he, " Thou hast a sour name, a bitter tongue, and a peppery temper, jade ; and the two last be not gifts o' the Lord."

" And thou," quoth she, " hast a mustard conceit, for right sure am I that 'tis big enough for a goose to roost in ! And whether th' Lord hath given it to thee or not, I'm glad I have 't not," quoth she; for she had heard it read, in some meeting whither her mother would sometimes take her, of how the fowls o' the air did lodge i' th' branches o' the mustard-plant. Well, by'r lay'kin, th' village hath ne'er for-

got that to this day, and that I'll prove
thee when we be through drinking!

What hath become o' her? Go to!
Sure thou knowest that? Well, well 'tis a
tale to make a play of. I've often thought,
had Master Shakespeare known of 't, how
he would 'a' fashioned it into a jolly play.
Tell thee of 't? What! art in earnest?
By the mass, then, thou must drink again.
Come, fill up, fill up. What there! a cup
o' the amber drink for Master Turnip!

Let me see: how old was th' lass when
thou didst set forth on thy jauntings?
Some two years, methinks. And she was
fourteen on the first day o' March i' that
year wherein she did sauce old Butter with
some o' 's own wit for gibing at her for a
tomboy. O' my word, man, th' old fellow,
was not far i' th' wrong. If e'er th' angel
o' life did make an error i' th' distributing
o' souls, 'twas on the night Keren was
brought into this world. And a say that
with a cause, moreover; for th' same

night, mark you, one Mistress Mouldy, over the way, was brought to bed o' a man-child. That's neither here nor there. Herein doth lie the singularity. That child did grow up to knit stockings i' th' door-way like any wench; Peter Mouldy's th' name, and a plays a part i' th' story I'm about to relate to thee. Ne'er in all thy travels hast thou e'er seen so crack-brain a wench as my Keren! Lord! it set thy head to swimming did she but enter a room. She had no more stability o' motion than a merry-go-round; and she was that brown, a bun looked pale i' th' comparison, when she did lift it to her mouth to eat it. A strapping jade, and strong as any lad o' her age i' th' village. In her seeming she took neither after her mother nor after me, though she was a comely wench as wenches go—hair as black as a January night in stormy weather, and eyes as big and as bright and as yellow (o' my word) — as yellow as two crown pieces!

They looked out from under her thick eye-
brows like sunlight peeping from a heavy
cloud. And she was made like a lad for
suppleness. Taller than her mother by
head and shoulders, and within a full inch
o' my forelock. By'r lay'kin! how she
could sing too! She would troll thee a
ditty i' th' voice o' a six-foot stripling, but
for a' that, as sweet as bells far away on a
still noon in summer-tide. And she was
always getting hold o' saucy songs, and putting them to tunes o' her own invention.
A could 'a' had aye the lads i' th' village,
had a wanted 'em; but, Lord! a had one
sweetheart one day, and another the next,
till they were one and all for murdering
or marrying her. But she would none o'
'em. 'Twas one summer's day, her mother
being gone to th' village, that she did set
about to brew some sack; and as she did
stand by the big pot while it cooled, to see
that naught fell into 't, up comes Master
Peter Mouldy with his knitting, and grins

at her across the caldron, after the fashion
o' a horse eating briers. She not noticing
him, quoth he,

"Good-morrow, sweet Mistress Lemon."

Saith she, not looking at him,

"Thou liest."

"How, mistress?" saith he, with his
mouth as wide as a church door on a
Sunday.

"Why, for calling a lemon sweet," saith
she, "when all the world doth know that it
is sour."

Thereat he did fall a-grinning again.

"Sweet, sweet mistress Keren," quoth he,
"'tis thee I praise, and not thy name. And
I will wager that thou art not sour, Mistress Keren."

"How wilt thou find out, either to lose
or to win thy wager?" quoth she.

"Thus!" quoth he. And, o' my word,
the homespun got his arms about her, knitting and all (though I would 'a' laid two
cows and a lamb they couldn't 'a' reached

about her pretty waist), and smacked her right heartily full on her red mouth.

Well, comrade, that something would happen I knew full well; but when she did up with him by the seat o' his breeches and the collar o' his jerkin, and did souse him head first into the pot o' sack, me-thought I would 'a' burst in sunder, like Judas Iscariot (meaning no blasphemy).

And when he was climbed out, splutter-ing and white with terror, she did fish out his hat with his big knitting-needles, and did set it upon his head, and did thrust him outside, and did shut the door in 's face. But never a word said she from first to last. Then methought in verity I would 'a' split in twain from top to toe, like the veil o' the temple (meaning no blasphemy, as I will swear on th' book). And when she caught sight o' me she too fell a-laugh-ing, and quoth she to me, "I have spoiled a good brew for thee, father, but 'twas worth the paying for." And therewith she did out with the worth o' the sack from her purse, which she always carried in her bosom, after a fashion inherited from her mother, and counted down the silver into my hand. I took it, for I ever strove to bring up my children in the ways o' honesty; and certes she had spoiled the contents o' the caldron by turning it into a bath-tub for Master Mouldy. Well, 'twas th' talk o' th' village for full a month; scarce did young Mouldy dare put out his nose from behind the lattice o' his mother's cottage. But th' other lads seemed to fall more daft about the lass than aye afore.

Now, my wife's sister had a daughter, called Ruth, and in all things was she most different from my Keren. A'd a head as yellow as Keren's eyes, and eyes as brown as Keren's skin, and a skin as white as Keren's teeth; and a was slim and tender-looking, like a primrose that hath but just ventured out on a day in early spring. Moreover, she was a timid, sweet-voiced creature—the kind o' wench that makes even a weak man feel strong, ye mind, comrade. But a was ne'er o'er-civil to my lass. Neither did Keren waste much love upon her; she said from th' very start that th' hussy had a sly tongue; "and a sly tongue," saith she, "doth ever mate with a false heart," saith she; "and from such a marriage what offspring can ye look for, unless it be for mischief?" saith she.

They had not much to do the one with the other, however, until the coming of Robert Hacket to Pebworth. And a was as fine a lad as e'er caused a lass to don her Sunday kirtle on a Saturday. 'Twas said as how he had met with Ruth while that she was on a visit to her aunt in Dancing Marston, and that he had come to Pebworth to wed with her. All would 'a' been well had not it come to Keren's ears how that Mistress Ruth said that she would bring Master Hacket to see her cousin Keren, but that she did not want her sweetheart to be out with her family ere that he had married into it; meaning neither more nor less than that my Keren was a shame unto her name by reason o' her romping ways.

"The cat!" quoth Keren, waxing as red as any damask rose for very anger; "the little, spiteful cat! But I'll cut her claws for her! Do thou bide and mark me, father. Ay, I'll serve her and her Robert in such wise they'll go to their graves remembering."

Now, 'twas the very next day that the lads and lasses o' the village did crown her harvest-queen, and all Bidford was out to see 't. And very queen she looked, too, borne aloft in a throne made all o' dark red roses, and her dark curls crowned with a wreath o' corn and o' poppies, that shined in the sunlight like to gold strewn all with rubies. She wore a new kirtle of white wool, and her brown throat rose from her white kerchief like as a frozen wood-dove's dusky breast doth peep from new-fallen snow.

And Mistress Ruth walked beside her as one o' her maids o' honor. And they twain did remind me of naught so much as of a lamb trotting by the side of a forest doe—the one so meek and white, and the other so free and brown, with great eyes ever moving, and head aloft.

There, moreover, walked Master Hacket. He was as brown as my Keren, and nearly half as tall again; and he had eyes like pools o' water under a night heaven, wherein two stars have drowned themselves, as 'twere, and brows as black and straight as a sweep o' cloud across an evening sky. Ruth walked at his side, all glittering with her unbound hair, like to a sunbeam that follows a dark stream. And I saw that they talked together, and nodded as though agreeing on something, and looked together at my lass where she sat on her flower-throne with her poppy-crown, and her lips like poppies. And all at once she turned and saw them, and her lips parted over her white teeth in a sudden smile, as when a kirtle o' red silk doth tear over a white petticoat beneath; and she turned away; but I could see that she laughed in her brown throat, as a bird sings sometimes for its own hearkening ere trolling for the whole forest. So I said to myself, "'Ware, 'ware, my little spring lamb; there is trouble ahead for thee. Thou wilt not win thy Boaz so easily as thou dost think, my little Ruth."

Now, when they were come to the fields, and the maids seated under some elm-trees, and all the lads fallen to 't with their sickles, while that they were reaping the glistening corn my Keren doth leap to her feet, and she calls out,

"I know not the name o' yonder man, but I do know that I can give him a lesson in reaping!"

So forthwith up jumps she, and, striding

out into the sunlit meadow, jerks young
Hacket's sickle from his hand, and, having turned back the sleeves o' her smock,
stands well upon her shapely legs and be-
gins to reap.

Now, methought I had ne'er in all my
life seen anything more pleasing to look
upon. The wind blew down her thick
locks about her, so that she was wrapped
in a mantle worthy any queen; while with
every sweep o' her strong brown arms the
tumbling grain did fall like gold about her,
so that she seemed to be trampling upon
her treasures after a manner truly royal.
Also a red came into her shadowy cheeks,
like as though a scarlet flower tossed into
a clear brown stream should rise slowly
upward beneath the limpid surface and
shine a-through. And all at once she
ceased, and came back towards the young
man, and returned his sickle unto him.
And she said, smiling,

" Take thou thy blade, for I have not

7

only reaped the grain, but I have reaped the reward of my bragging as well." And, behold! when I was come up to them with a drink o' water in a gourd, there was the blood falling down upon her white kirtle, as though the poppies in her crown had melted in the sunlight and did stain her garment.

He did cry out, saying, " O' my word, lass, thou art deeply hurt. Let me but look at it."

She saith unto him (winding her arm about in her long hair), " Nay, 'tis nothing, and belike if thou look upon it 'twill spoil thy dinner: so here's to thy health, and my father will bind it for me."

Then, when we were retired again into the shade, and I had torn a strip off of her kirtle wherewith to stanch the blood, she laughed outright, and saith,

" By my troth, father! I do verily believe thou thinkest me awkward without a purpose."

" Purpose !" saith I; for I could not believe my ears. " How dost thou mean—
purpose ?"

" That's neither here nor there," saith
she, still laughing. " But I'll lay thee my
heifer, father, that Mistress Ruth's sweetheart cometh on the morrow to inquire
after Mistress Ruth's cousin Keren."

Wherewith she did make me a deep
courtesy, and did get her back to the other
lasses ere I could reply.

Well, as I live, and must some day die,
and do hope when I do die to get to
heaven, I was so taken aback with the
hussy's cunning I could do naught but
stand and stare after her for some minutes.

And on the morrow he did come, and
on the day after that he came, and yet a
third day and he was under my roof again.

Then saith my wife, after that his third
visit was o'er, and speaking to Keren as
she sat spinning i' th' door-way,

"Happuch," saith she, "thou art serving thy cousin Ruth a very jade's trick."

Then, hearing as how she did call her "Happuch," I did prick up my ears, as 'twere; for I knew there was anger brewing.

"Thou art very free with thy words to-day, mother," quoth the maid, a-spinning very quickly.

"Not so free as thou art with thy favors to the sweetheart o' another lass," replied her mother.

"How dost thou know he is the sweetheart o' another lass?" saith Keren.

"If an he be not," quoth her mother, who, though not half so big as her child, was in nowise less valiant—"if an he be not," quoth she, "'tis time he were."

"And for why?" saith Keren.

"Thou knowest as well as I do, Happuch," saith my wife; whereat up started my crack-brain in a fine fury.

"Why wilt thou call me that vile name, when thou knowest how it maddens me?"

saith she, hurling her spindle upon the floor, and tightening both her pretty hands so that they looked like balls o' her own brown yarn.

"For that I am not pleased with thee, Happuch," saith her mother, with all composure, looking at the linen as she washed it, with her head cocked to one side.

"There again!" shouted my wildfire, stamping with her foot. "Why didst thou not call me Beelzebub and have done with 't?"

"For the reason," quoth her mother, calmly, "that neither Beel nor Zebub is a suiting name for a woman, and, furthermore, that thou art not the Devil, though thou dost act like him on occasions."

"Wife, wife," put in I, seeing that the girl was like to split with rage, "speak gentler to Keren."

"To Happuch," saith she.

"Speak gentler to the girl," saith I, hoping to compromise, as 'twere.

"Happuch," saith my wife again.

"Well, well," saith I, still hoping to split the difference, so that I would have neither my wife nor my daughter upon me, "if thou wouldst only speak gentler to Keren-Happuch, thou—"

"To Happuch," saith my wife a third time; whereat the lass did bounce out o' the house without more ado, and spent that night with a friend o' her own, by name one Mistress Meg Titmouse.

"Wife," saith I unto her later, hoping to draw her into converse concerning Keren, so that I might reason with her as to her treatment o' th' lass — "wife," saith I, amiably, and, as I thought, in a manner most winsome, "wherefore didst thou speak to Keren as thou didst this morning?"

"I spake to Happuch," saith my wife, "because I did choose so to do. And as for the why o' that wherefore, though thou shouldst smirk till doomsday like a dog scratching his ear, ne'er wilt thou get it out o' me!"

Then saith I, being justly angered, as I think thou wilt admit, comrade—saith I,

"Thou art welcome to keep thy counsel!" saith I.

And I followed the example set me by my vixen, and did spend more than half the night at this very tavern.

Well, the next morning, as I did pass out on my way to my forge, whom should I see in the garden but my Keren and Master Robert Hacket! and if e'er a woman was possessed o' a devil, 'twas just that lass o' mine then, comrade. She had caused young Hacket to climb up into a pear-tree, and while that he was up there she did bear away the ladder by which he had mounted, and she saith to him,

"Now, Master Robin, I am going to sing thee a song. Wilt thou listen?"

"With all my heart," saith he. So he leaned on his elbow, stretched out like a young panther along the limb o' th' tree, and looked down on her. Now, as I live, down went that jade on her knees in the grass, and she lifts up her two pretty hands to him as though in prayer, and thus sings she (I knew the song by heart):

"'Listen, Robin, while I woo.
　This world's stale with repetition:
I'll not do as others do;
　Haste thee, love, to my tuition.
Robin, I'll make love to you,
As men to other maidens do.

"'Oh, what eyes my Robin hath!
　April fields own no such blue;
In the luscious aftermath
　There's no flower so fair to view.
Robin, Robin, hear me woo.
All my soul's in love with you!

"'Robin, will you marry me?—
　Thus upon my knees I sue:
O' my word I'll harry thee
　Like as men their sweethearts do.
Robin, as I live I'm true:
Will you wed me, Robin?—Will you?'"

Now, what chanced thereupon I think
thou wilt agree with me, comrade, in saying it did but serve her right. Down falls
he like a ripe pomewater at her side, and
takes her about the waist, and sets his
mouth to hers (all in a twink, comrade;
thou hadst not time to shape thy mouth
for a whistle ere 'twas all done, or verily
my mouth had given forth something besides whistling), and saith he,

"That will I, lass; an' if thou be not
my wife ere that snail-coming new moon
doth thrust out her horns, my name is not
Hacket, nor will thine be!"

Now, comrade, though it doth shame me
verily so to speak o' mine own flesh, I saw
by her pretending to push him away that
she did mightily relish his kisses; for, by
my troth! had she sought to scuffle with
him 'twould 'a' been as snug an encounter
as when day and night wrestle for the last
bit o' a June sky.

And she saith to him, feigning to scowl,

"How now, thou rapscallion! dost thou dare?"

"Ay, ay," quoth he, "in verity I do!" quoth he. And in verity a did, too.

But just as I was consulting with the Lord how to act, He having had even a greater experience with wayward children than myself (may He pardon me if I be too free with His holy name!)— just, I say, as I was asking Him to show me in what wise to proceed, up goes her hand, and she gives him a sound cuff o' th' ear (young Hacket's ear—not the Lord's; may He pardon me if so it sounded), and she saith,

"Take that for striving to make a fool out o' an honest girl! I know thy goings on with Ruth Visor," saith she. "Thou'lt ne'er blind me with thy pretty speecheries." And a was o'er th' palings and out o' sight like a wind-blown leaf.

Then did young Hacket come to th' fence and lean upon it with both his arms, and support his chin with a thumb on either side o't, and saith he,

"Methinks she'd 'a' made a better warrior than a wife," saith he; "but when she hath ta'en off the edge o' her warlike spirit in fighting for her freedom," saith he, "why, then," saith he, "I'll marry her!" So saith he—every word o't. By my troth, comrade, an I had not had so much the advantage by having my nippers in my hand, I would 'a' thrashed him then and there. But, "fair play" being my motto, and having my nippers, as I saith, I forbore; yea, I forbore, and walked away unseen of him. And, o' my word, I was much angered with myself for not being more angry with th' wench.

"For," saith I, out loud, that I might be impressed by the sound as well as by the knowledge o' th' fact — "for," saith I, a-hammering away on a shoe for Joe Pebbles's brown nag King Edward (though I had often reasoned with Joe on account o' th' name, first because o' its irreverence, second on account o' th' horse not being that kind o' a horse, as 'twas a mare)— "for," saith I, as I made th' shoe, saith I, "'tis sure a great wickedness to steal a lass's sweetheart away from her!" saith I. And so 'twas; but, for all I could do, I could not feel angered with the hussy.

But that day when she did fetch me my dinner, being finished, I did pull down th' sleeves o' my shirt, and wiped off my leathern apron, and quoth I to her,

"Lass, come here and sit upon my knee."

So she comes right willingly, being fond o' me to an extent that did oft seem to astony the mother that bore her (seeing that *she* was fond o' naught save her own way); she comes, and she perches upon my knee (as sometimes thou shalt see a hawk rest wings on a bull's back), and she kittles my throat with her long brown fingers, and hugs me about the neck (the jade! a knew I was for scolding her), and saith she,

"Well, father, here be I." Methinks I can hear her say it now, as soft as any little toddler come for a kiss. "Here be I," she saith; and with that she fills all my face with her curls (the jade! a saw that in my eye which a did not care to face). "Here be I," saith she.

"Ay," saith I, speaking in a gruff voice; "and now that here thou be," saith I, "I'll tell thee what I want of thee."

"Thou canst want naught that I will not do," saith she. (The jade! a had a way with her to 'a' made Bess herself yearn for matrimony.) But I was stanch; I was stanch, comrade. Saith I,

"Methinks thy mother was right to speak to thee as yesternight she did," saith I; "for I saw thee strive to graft a pear-tree with a branch o' th' tree o' knowledge," saith I.

"Then," saith she, hot as my forge all in a breath, and bouncing from my knee— "then thou wast an eavesdropper!" saith she.

"Even as the Lord afore me," saith I, not over-pleased at her sauciness. "And being in some sort thy Creator, and thou having set up for thyself an Eden in my garden," saith I, "who hath a greater right than I to watch over thee?" saith I.

Then she not answering me, thus did I continue:

"Why dost thou not take unto thyself an husband," quoth I, "to do both thyself and thy parents a credit?"

"Show me such an one," saith she, "and I do promise thee to wed him."

"There, then," quoth I, "is Davy Short-hose, the poulterer—"

"A bangled-eared buffoon as ever lived!" quoth she; "and a fool into the bargain."

"So be it," saith I; for I was set upon keeping my temper. "What dost thou say to Beryamen Piggin, the brewer?"

"A say if ever a piggin was in sore need o' a new link, 'tis that one," saith she. "And, what's more, I'll not serve for 't," saith she.

" How, then, of Nanfan Speckle, the tanner?"

"A's as pied as a's name," quoth she, "both soul and body."

" There be Jezreel Spittlewig, the joiner."

" Methinks," quoth she, " if a'd do a little joining to a's own shackling body, a might hold together long enough to go through the marriage ceremony," saith she. " Howbeit, I'm not a-sure of 't."

" Well, then, Jack Stirthepot, the chairmender."

"A'd have to stir th' pot with a witch ere a brewed a wedding with me," quoth she.

" What sayest to Reuben Puff, the tinker?"

" If I say so much as a word to any one o' em," cried she, snatching up the pail wherein she had brought my victuals, "may thy first grandchild be born without a tongue!" saith she. And out she went.

Then quoth I to myself, quoth I, "Lemon," quoth I, "the jade's in love with th' crack—no more, no less." And I said further, said I, "Bodykins!" said I, a-shoeing of King Edward with all my might, "by cock and pye!" said I, "an a wants him let a have him. 'Tis more than his desert, I'll warrant," so quoth I. "And as for Dame Visor's hussy, let her learn to bridle her tongue," quoth I. And 'twas just here that wench Keren did creep up and take me about the neck, as I was a-filing of King Edward's hoof.

"Father," saith she, "I cry thee pardon if I have sauced thee; but dost not mind the rhyme thou art so fond of?—

"'Shoe the horse, and shoe the mare,
But let the little colt go bare.'

Seek not to chide me, father, and ne'er will my heels bring hurt to any."

Then off was she again ere I had spat forth my mouthful o' nails to answer her.

But that evening as I came home, about

the going down o' th' sun, I did hear voices i' th' kitchen, and, looking in at th' window, behold, there was that hussy Ruth a-plucking of Keren by th' kirtle, and Keren a-holding of a pan o' milk above her head, as though she had half a mind to souse her cousin in 't.

And saith she, "Get to thy feet, wench. This is neither a church, nor am I th' Lord."

But th' girl (who seemed to be in trouble o' some sort) fell a-sobbing, and saith she,

"Cousin, cousin, I know I have used thee ill, but all my joy is in him. If thou takest him from me, better didst thou take my life, for he is more to me than life."

Then quoth my lass, "Shame on thee to say it o' any man, worthy or unworthy!"

"Oh, shame enough have I, cousin!" quoth the poor wench—"shame to 'a' lost him, and shame that I should plead with another to give him back to me!"

"Go to!" saith Keren; "go to! I have not got him to give him back to thee."

8

"Thou hast!" saith Ruth; "thou hast!—he is thine, soul and body—soul and body! And thou dost not care; and I care—oh, I care so that I know not how to word it!"

(Every word that passed between 'em is as clear in my mind as though 'twere but yesterday it all happened.)

"I say shame on thee to say so," saith my lass again.

But the wench still hung about her, and would not let go, and she saith,

"Oh, cousin, cousin, cousin, doth it not show thee in what straits I am, that I come to thee for succor? Rather had I died, one week agone, than ask thee for thy hand though I were drowning. And sure 'tis less than thy hand for which I ask thee now, sith it be for a man who is less to thee than the littlest finger on that hand, but who is more to me than the heart in my wretched body! And a had vowed to wed me; and 'twas next month we were to be wed; and all so happy—my father and

my mother so pleased, and his folks do like
me well; and my wedding-gown all sewn
and lain away, and the ribbons for my
shoes, and some kickshaws for th' new
house; and all we so glad, and all going
so smooth, and we twain so loving; for,
oh, he did love me the once! he did love
me the once! And now—now—now—"
And here did she fall a-weeping in such
wise that never another word could she
say. And she sate down on the kitchen
floor, and hid all her pretty head (for
pretty 'twas, though I liked her not)—hid
it all in the skirt o' her kirtle."

Then stood my lass quite still, and her
face like the milk in her pan, and she looks
down on th' hussy, as a horse might look
down on a kitten which it hath unwitting
trampled on, and she saith,

"I would I knew whether or no thou
speakest the truth!"

Then saith the wench, a-reaching up her
clasped hands to heaven—saith she,

"May God forever curse me an I do not !"

"Take not God's name in vain," saith my lass, sharply, and went and set down her pan o' milk on the cupboard. And again she stands, slowly wiping her hands on her apron, and looking down at th' girl, who hath once more covered all her face in her petticoat; and by-and-by she saith to her,

"What is 't thou wouldst have me do?"

"Give me back my Robin! give me back my Robin!" saith the maid.

"Thou art welcome to him for me," saith Keren.

Then fell the maid a-weeping more bitterly than ever, and she huddled herself on the hard floor, like a young bird that hath fallen out o' its nest, and sobbed piteously. And presently gets she to her feet without a word, still a-hiding of her face in her kirtle, and turns to go, a-feeling her way with one o' her little hands. But when she hath reached th' door, and hath got one foot on the threshold, up strides that lass o' mine, and, taking her by the arm, swings her back into th' room; and she makes her sit down on a settle and take down her kirtle from her face. And while she is snooding up her ruffled locks, she saith unto her,

"Thou art a little fool to cry so; dost hear? What! at it again? Well, well, God patience me! What's a body to do with such a little ninny? There! dry your eyes. Ye shall have your Robin, never fear. God-a-mercy! at what art blubbering now?" But down slipped Ruth on her knees, and caught Keren about hers, and she saith unto her,

"Heaven bless thee! thou art a good woman! May Heaven forgive me for all such words as e'er I have said against thee! Bless thee! bless thee!"

"Bodykins!" saith my lass (having learned some round oaths from me, I do grieve to say)—"bodykins!" saith she, "wilt a-hear th' lass? I say scamper, scamper; my father 'll be coming home to sup erelong, and I would not he found thee thus. Away with thee! and fret no more: dost hear? If I hear that thou hast moped any further from this hour on, I'll not answer either for my doings or for those o' others: dost hear? Now scamper!" And scamper a did, like a hare with th' hounds upon 't.

So full was I o' praising my lass on her good 'havior that I had got me from th' lattice and was half in at the door ere I saw what had befallen.

There was my madcap, comrade, down on her knees afore the settle, wi' both hands gripped in her thick locks, and her head bent forward on th' wooden seat; and she made no sound, neither uttered she any word, but a shook like water when a heavy weight rolls past. And a drew long breaths ever and anon, like one that hath been half drowned and is coming back to life. And I knew then, I knew then, comrade. I had thought a loved th' boy; and I knew then. So I got me out, without making any clatter, and I sat me down on a bench outside th' kitchen door to think 't over; and, by cock and pye, man, ne'er a thought could I think for th' tears in my eyes. Th' poor lass! th' poor lass! It fetches th' salt into my een now to think on 't. Well, well, what's past is past, and God himself cannot undo 't; and what's coming's coming, and God wunnot hinder it an he could; so there's an end on 't. Fill up, man, fill up! What there, I say! Joel, I say! A quart o' sack for Master Turnip.

Well, when I had thought it well o'er, I did determine to say naught to th' lass whatsoever; neither did I; but meseems I was bound to o'erhear heart-breaking words atween somebody, for th' very next day, as I was henting th' style as leads into th' lane (thou knowest the lane I mean, comrade: 't lies atween Cowslip Meadow and th' pool i' th' hollow—Sweethearts' Way, they call 't)—well, as I was getting o'er th' style—as I had just got me o'er by one leg, after this fashion, ye mind; as though this chair here were th' style, and yonder chimney-place th' lane— Sweethearts' Way, ye mind—well, as I was half over, and Mumble, th' turnspit pup, half under, as 'twere, I heard voices— voices, comrade—one o' them th' voice o' that lass o' mine, and t'other th' voice o' young Hacket.

"Here be a coil," say I. "What's to do?"

Now the pup seemed to be filled with the spirit o' th' Lord all on a sudden, after th' fashion o' th' talking jackass i' th' Scriptures; for if a didna talk a did th' next thing to 't—a tried to. And after pulling at my heels like as though a fiend had got him, a scuttles into th' thicket, for no cause, as I could see, but to give me th' benefit o' example. So in goes I after him. Scarce was I settled, with a bramble down th' back o' my neck, and some honey-bees at work too nigh to my legs for my peace o' mind, when they come, and both a-chattering at th' same time like two magpies with slit tongues.

"Thou didst!" quoth he. "That did I not!" quoth she. "Thou didst, and I can prove 't on thee!" quoth he, louder than afore. "I tell thee I did not, and thou canst sooner prove that Bidford Mill turns the Avon than that I did!" quoth she. "Wilt thou stand there and tell me i' th' eyes that thou hast so oft looked love into," quoth he, like a man choked with spleen—"I say, wilt thou, Keren Lemon, stand there and face me, Robert Hacket, and say thou hast ne'er given me reason to believe that thou didst love me?" quoth he. "No more cause than I've given to twenty better than thee!" quoth she. "Shame on thee to say 't, thou bold faced

jig!" saith he; "shame on thee, I say! and
so will say all honest folk when I tell
'em o' 't." "An thou tell it, the more fool
thou," saith she; and a draws up her red
lips into a circle as though a'd had a draw-
string in 'em, and a stands and looks at
him as a used to stand and look at her
dam when she chid her for a romp. Then
all on a sudden, with such a nimbleness
as took away my breath and drove all
thoughts o' brambles and honey-bees clean
out o' my pate, he jumps aside o' her, and
gets her about th' middle, as he did that
day under th' pear-tree, and quoth he,
"Lass," quoth he, "dunnot break my heart!
dunnot break th' heart that loves ye more
than a' that's in the earth, or th' heavens
above, or th' waters below! Say ye love
me, and ha' done with 't."

Then gives she up herself to him for
one beat o' her own breaking heart, the
poor madcap, and she leans on him with
all her pretty self, as though begging him

to take her against her own will, and then
a cry breaks from her, half human, and half
like th' cry o' a hurt beast, and she saith,

"Shame on ye, shame on ye, to forsake
th' lass ye ha' sworn to wed! Get thee
back to her straightway, or ne'er look me
i' th' face again!" And she leaps back from
him, and points with her arm—as stiff and
steady as th' tail o' a sportsman's dog—
towards th' village, and she saith again,
"Get thee back to her; get thee back to
Ruth Visor, and wed with her ere this
month be out o' the year!"

Then lifts he his sullen head, and looks
at her from under his brows like a smitten
blood-hound. And he saith back o' his
clamped teeth, like as 'twere a dog gnarl-
ing in his throat, "curse ye for a false
jade!" saith he; "Curse ye for as black-
hearted a jade as e'er set an honest man
on th' road to hell!" And he turned, and
cleared th' style with one hand on 't, and
went his ways.

And th' lass stood and looked after him as still as though she were turned into a pillar o' summat, after th' manner o' th' woman i' th' holy book, and both, her hands grasping her breast. But anon there comes a trouble o'er her face, like as when a little wind doth run across a gray pool at eventide, and her lips begin to tremble, like as though some red flower a-growing on th' bank was shaken by 't, and her eyes all full o' woe, like th' eyes o' some dumb thing as cannot word its sorrow; and all at once she falls upon her knees, and thence upon her forehead on the ground, and afterwards to her whole length, with her strong hands grasping th' flowers and grass on either side o' her, and tearing them up with th' crackling noise that a horse makes when 't grazes. But no sound escapes her, whether a sigh or a groan. Well, well, comrade, I cry thee patience if I do stumble here a bit: I cannot think on 't now without a tightness i' my

throat, any more than a man can think o'
th' day his first child was born to him without his heart leaping hot in 's throat like
the flame to th' bellows. Well, well! Fill
up, I say; fill up. Remember th' old days,
when thou wast more ale-washed than th'
bottle itself. Where be I i' th' narrative?
Yea, yea, 'tis there—'tis there; I mind me
o't now.

No sound 'scaped her, but presently she
lifts herself up upon her knees again, with
such heaviness as a horse overburdened
doth get him to his feet, and she holds out
both her arms i' th' direction where th' lad
hath vanished, wi' th' grass and flowers yet
fast in her clinched hands; and she saith
twice, i' th' voice o' a woman in travail,

"Never will he know, never will he
know," she saith; and then, "Oh, God!"
she saith, a-lifting her hands again to her
breast. "Summat's broke here," she saith,
full meek, like a body that's looked a many
time on pain—"summat's broke, summat's

broke," o'er and o'er again, as though she would use herself to th' sound, as 'twere. Then all at once did a deep cry break from her. "God, O God," she saith, "show me how to bear 't! My God, my God, show me how to bear 't." And she got to her feet, and sped down th' lane like one blind, running first into th' hawthorn bushes o' this side, then into th' quickset hedge o' th' other, and tearing out her loosened tresses on th' low-hanging branches o' th' pear-trees, so that I traced her by her hair i' th' twigs, like as thou wouldst trace any poor lost lamb by its wool on the brambles. Now, it did almost break my own heart to say naught to her concerning all o't, but I knew that 'twould but grieve without comforting her; and rather would I 'a' had my old heart split in twain than bring one more ache into her true breast. So naught say I. Never a word, comrade, from then till now have I e'er said to her about that time.

Well, for all 's fine talk, Master Hacket went no more to hell than do any other men that marry—an' less than some, seeing as how a did not marry a scold, which (God forgive me, or her, or both o' us) I have done. Yea, comrade, I will commemorate this our first meeting in eight years by confessing to thee that my wife (in thy ear, comrade)—that my wife was a scold. Sometimes I do verily think as how women like Mistress Lemon be sent unto men to keep 'em from pondering too heavily concerning the absence o' marriage in heaven. By cock and pye, man, as I live, I do honestly believe that I would rather be a bachelor in hell, than the husband o' Mistress Lemon in heaven!

But to come back to th' lass. And, now that I think o' th' lass, comrade, I am not so sure that a scolding wife is not well paid for by a duteous daughter. Nay, I am sure o't. Methinks I would 'a' been wed twice, and each time to a shrew, could

I but 'a' had my Keren o' one o' 'em. Ay, even so, even so.

Well, as I said—or as I meant to say—Master Hacket wedded th' Visor hussy within two weeks o' th' day whereon he and my Keren had 't so fierce i' Sweethearts' Way. And therein are two meanings: they fell out, as is the way with sweethearts, and they fell out i' th' lane so called.

Well, well, let me crack a quart o' sack with thee, comrade, and a joke at th' same time.

A married Ruth Visor, and they went to Lunnon Town. And on th' night o' their wedding, as I sat by the fireside i' th' kitchen a-mending my tools (for 'twas on a Saturday night), and Keren abed, and Mistress Lemon a-peeling o' leather-jackets to make th' Sunday pie,

"Wife," saith I to her (a-mending my tools, as I ha' said), " wife, "quoth I, " would 'twere our lass were wed to-day!"

" For why ?" saith she. No more, no less.

" For why ?" saith I. " For the why I think a lass is happier wed to th' man she loves," saith I.

"'Tis not so I've found it," quoth she, a-peeling of an apple so that thou couldst 'a' put his whole coat back and not 'a' known 't had e'er come off.

Then quoth I, a-chuckling in my throat at having so snared her, " Right glad am I to find out that thou lovest me !" quoth I.

" If thou'st found out that," quoth she, " thou'rt greater than Columbus," quoth she, " for thou'st discovered something that never was," quoth she.

" Bodykins, woman !" saith I, a-losing of my temper — " then for what didst thou marry me ?"

" For a fool," quoth she. " And I will say as I ha' got the full o' my bargain," quoth she.

Whereat so wroth was I that I said naught, knowing that if I did open my lips

9

or move my hand 'twould be to curse her with th' one and cuff her with t'other.

By-and-by saith she, "And where, by'r lay'kin, wilt thou find a man good enough in thy eyes for th' lass?" saith she.

"Not on earth," quoth I. "Neither in this land nor that other across the sea," quoth I.

"Ay, ay," quoth she. "Very like thou wouldst háve th' wench to wed with an angel," quoth she; "to have all thy grand-children roosting on a gold bar, and their dad a-teaching of 'em how to use their wings," quoth she. "Or with one o' th' red men i' th' new country, to have them piebald red and white, like a cock-horse at Banbury Cross," quoth she. And with that up she gets, and flings the apple-parings into th' fire, and gets her to bed without more ado. Whereupon day doth again find me i' this very tavern.

Well, well, a year had passed, and things were jogging very peaceful like, and Keren

settled down as quiet as a plough-broken
mare, when one day as I sit i' th' kitchen,
while th' lass mends my apron, there comes
a fumbling at th' latch like as though a
child made shift to open it. Then quoth
I, " Belike 'tis little Marjory Pebble, or one
o' the Mouldy lads over th' way ;" for the
babes all loved Keren, and, now that she
was waxed so quiet, th' lads left her more
to herself, and she would sit on th' bench
by the cottage door and make little kickshaws by th' hour — elder - wood whistles,
and dolls o' forked radishes, and what not.
So quoth I, " Belike 'tis little Marjory Pebble," quoth I, and th' lass having her lap
full o' my apron, I went and opened th'
door. And there, comrade, a-kneeling in
th' grass outside, with her head all hid in
her kirtle, as she had kneeled two years
agone on t'other side o' that very door,
was Mistress Ruth Hacket ; and she was
a-sobbing as though her heart would break.
And while I stand staring, ere I could find

a word to my tongue, comes that lass o' mine and pushes me aside like as though I had been little Marjory Pebble—ha! ha! And down goes she on her knees beside th' lass, and gets an arm about her, and presses down her head, all hid as 'tis in her kirtle, against her breast, and she saith to her,

"What troubles thee? Tell Keren, honey. So so! What troubles thee? Tell Keren."

And from beneath her kirtle th' poor jade sobs out, "He's gone! he's gone! he's gone! They've taken him to work on th' big seas—and our child not yet born—and me so ailing; and, oh! I want to die! I want to die!"

Then saith that lass o' mine, saith she, "Father, do thou fetch some o' th' birch wine out o' th' cupboard and bring it to me in a cup;" and to the girl she saith, "Come, then; come, then," like as though she had been coaxing some little spring lambkin to follow her unto its dam; and she half pulls and half carries th' wench into th' house, and seats her on a low stool i' th' chimney-corner, and kneels down aside of her. And when I be come with th' drink, she takes the cup out o' my hand, and makes th' wench drink 't, holding it to her lips with one hand, while with the other she cossets her hair and cheek. And, by-and-by, seeing myself forgotten, I do withdraw into the room beyond, and wait till I be called, that th' lasses may have 't out together.

Now, Ruth's folks were aye so poor that scarce could they keep clothes on their backs and food i' their bellies; and it hath some time occurred to me how that the Lord might 'a' given such as could not provide for themselves a coat o' wool or o' hair that would 'a' covered their bodies, after the manner of a sheep or goat — the righteous being clad i' th' first fashion, and the wicked after th' last.

Well, well, I must on. I see thou art

waxing restless, comrade. Not so? Well, drink, drink, then, that I may feel thou art well occupied while that my old tongue wags.

So poor, then, were Ruth's folks that I said to myself, said I, "What i' th' name o' pity," so saith I — "what i' th' name o' pity is to become o' the poor lass?" But I had scarce asked myself th' question when my lass answers it for me.

"Father," saith she, a-coming and standing afore me, with the empty cup turning on her long fingers — "father," saith she, keeping those gold-colored eyes o' hers on mine (methinks they were coined o' th' same wedge as her heart o' gold) — "father," saith she, just so, "considering all things," saith she, "I'm going to keep th' lass in my room till her child be born," so saith she.

Then saith I, pulling her down into my arms, "Lass," saith I, "verily do I believe that not only is every hair o' thy sweet head numbered, but that each one is blessed with a separate blessing!" And what with my love for her, and my admiring of her goodness, and my pride in her, and what with her pity for the poor girl in th' other room, we did shed enough tears between us to ha' o'erflowed th' empty cup in her hands.

So she held me about th' neck with both arms, and like to ha' run me mad with kissing th' back o' my neck (for I was e'er one o' your ticklish sort). I stood it bravely, however, seeing how she loved me, and kissed her too whensoever I could get a chance for th' tightness o' her hugging. And so we settled it. But Mistress Lemon was yet to be consulted.

Ready enough was I to shift that job on my lass's broad shoulders (seeing as how a reputation for courage with his wife is ne'er believed o' a man, at any rate, and as how th' wench had a way o' managing her mother which sure none could 'a' had that were not of her own flesh). And that night, when her mother was returned from a round o' gossiping, th' lass tells her all (having i' th' mean time put Ruth to bed atween her own sheets). Well, ne'er saw I my wife in such a rage.

"What!" saith she, "thou hast ta'en it on thyself to offer my bread and meat to a good-for-naught hussy as ne'er had a civil word for any o' us! Thou hast given her bed-room under my roof without so much as 'by your leave!' Thou godless hussy, thou! Where be th' jade? I say, where be she? Where be she?"

"Where thou shalt not come at her in thy present humor, mother," saith the lass, standing with one arm reached out across the door-way, like as though in verity she had been the mother and her dam a naughty child.

"How? Dost word me? dost word me?" saith my wife. "How? dost take any stray cat to kitten in my house an' then word me too?"—so saith she.

Then saith th' lass, "Well can I understand," saith she, "how, if thou canst speak
i' this fashion o' thy sister's child, thou canst
also speak to thy own as sure no mother
e'er spoke ere this." Then, changing all
suddenly her tone, and dropping down her
arm from the door, "Go an thou like," saith
she, "to abuse the poor creature who hath
come to ask thy help in time o' trouble;
but just so surely as thou dost turn her out
o' door to lie i' th' straw like any common
callet, just so sure do I follow her, to fare
as she fares, and all the village shall know
what thou hast done."

Then for some minutes did they twain
stand and gaze upon one another, and at
last down flumps my wife into a chair, as
though she would break it in pieces for
very rage; but being waxed sulky, and her
own wrath cowed, as 'twere, by her daughter's more righteous wrath, she saith nothing more of 't, good or bad.

In three weeks' time th' child is born,

and as sound and as pretty a babe as e'er I clapt eyes on, and Keren a-dangling of him as natural as though she herself had been a mother, time and again.

"What say'st thou now, lass?" quoth she. "Wilt trust Keren after this?"

"Is he sound, verily?" saith the poor little dame, looking shyly upon him.

"Never a spot so big as the splash on a guinea-flower!" saith Keren. "And ears like sea-shells."

So, after a-kissing of them both, and th' top o' th' babe's head (as 'twas permitted me to do), I steals out and leaves them together.

Well, ne'er saw thou a child grow as did that child. Meseemed he sprouted like corn after a rain; and in five months a was waxed so strong a could stand on 's feet a-holding to his mother's kirtle. But, strange to say or not, as thou wilt have 't, he did seem to love Keren more than he did th' mother that bore him, a-crying for

her did she but so much as turn her back,
and not sleeping unless that she would
croon his lullabies to him. Mayhap it was
because her strong arms and round bosom
made a more cosey nest for him than did
th' breast and arms o' his little dam; but
so was 't, and nearly all o' her time did th'
lass give to him. Neither did it seem to
rouse aught o' jealousy in Ruth's heart:
she was too busy a-looking for th' return
o' 's father to bother her pretty pate o'er-
much concerning him. And she would sit
and talk o' Robin, and o' Robin's goodness, and o' Robin's sweet ways and words
and doings, until I thought sometimes my
poor lass's heart would just break within
her, if 't had not been broken already these
two years. And one day, as she kneels
beside th' cradle — Ruth having gone to
see her folks for th' day—I come in un-
known to her, and stand to watch th' pretty sight. There kneels she, and Ruth's
red shawl o'er her head to please th' child

(Keren ne'er had any bright colors o' her own those days)—there kneels she, I say, beside the cradle, and kittles him with her nimble fingers, and digs him i' th' ribs after a fashion that would sure 'a' run me crazy (though it hath ne'er yet been proven what a young babe cannot endure at the hands o' women), and punches and pokes and worries him, for all th' world like a kitten worrying a flower. And he, lying on his back, kicks with both feet at her face, and winds all his hands in her long hair, and laughs, and bubbles, and makes merry, after the fashion o' a spring stream among many stones. And by-and-by a change falls o'er her, and she waxes very solemn, and sits down on th' floor by th' edge o' th' cradle, with one arm upon 't and her head on her hand, and she looks at the babe. In vain doth he clutch at her hair and at her kerchief, and reach, with pretty broken murmurings, as of water through crowding roots, after his little bare toes: never so much as a motion makes she towards him. But at last up gets she to her knees, and takes him fiercely into her strong hands, and holds him off at arm's-length, looking at him; and she saith in a deep voice (such as I had not heard her use for two years), saith she, " For that thou art not mine," saith she, " I hate thee; but—" and here came a change o'er all her face and voice and manner, like as when April doth suddenly wake in the midst o' a wintry day in springtide—" but," saith she, "for that thou art his, I love thee!" And she took him to her bosom, and bowed down her head over him so that he was hidden all in her long hair; but the bright shawl covered it, so that, what with her stooping and the hiding of her tresses, a body coming in suddenly at the door might 'a' easily mistaken her for Ruth.

It was thus with th' man who at that moment strode past me and caught up child and woman into his embrace. " I

have come back to thee," he said—" I have
come back to thee. Look up, wife! Ruth,
look up!" But when she did look up, and
he saw her face as white as morning, and
her hair as black as night, and her tall
figure like to a young elm-tree—ay, when
she looked up, ne'er saw I a man not dead
seem so like death. He drops down his
arms from about them, as though smitten
from behind by a sword, and he staggers
and leans against th' table, and lets fall his
head upon his breast, staring straight in
front o' him. But she stands looking upon
him. And I got me out with all speed;
so ne'er knew I more o' what passed between 'em, saving that he did take away
Ruth with him th' next day, and she as
happy as a bird whose mate hath come
back to 't with the springtide. But a knew
how that my lass had taken his wife into
her bed, and nursed her through her sick-
ness night and day, after the hard words
he had spoken unto her and the ill names

he had called her. And that was all I
cared to know. He had set th' iron in
my lass's heart, and now 'twas in his own;
and for th' rust, it did but hurt him more.
Ay, ay, comrade, thou knowest what I do
mean.

Well, the winter passed, and spring
came on again, and 'twas in the May o'
that year that I did break my hammer-arm.
God above us only knows what would 'a'
befallen us had 't not been for my Keren.
Wilt believe 't? (but then I think thou'lt
believe a'most anything o' that lass o' mine
now — eh, comrade?) — th' lass did set to
work, and in two weeks' time a was as
good a farrier as was e'er her daddy afore
her. Bodykins, man! thou shouldst 'a'
seen her at it: clad from throat to feet
she was in a leathern apron, looking as like
mine own as though th' mare's skin where-
of mine was fashioned had, as 'twere, foal-
ed a smaller one for th' lass—ha! ha!—and
her sleeves rolled up from her brown arms,

and th' cords a-standing out on them like th' veins in a horse's shoulder. And so would she stand, and work th' bellows at th' forge, until, what with th' red light from the fire on her face, and on her hair, and on her bare arms, I was minded o' th' angel that walked i' the fiery furnace with th' men in holy writ. And when a pounded away at a shoe, and her young arm going like a flail—chink, chank—chink, chank—and th' white spatters o' hot iron flying this way and that from th' anvil, me-seemed 'twas as though Dame Venus (for thou knowest how in th' masque twelve year gone this Yuletide 'twas shown as how a great dame called Venus did wed wi' a farrier called Vulcan—I wot thou rememberest?)—as though Dame Venus had taken away her hammer from her goodman Vulcan to do 's work for him. By my troth, 'twas a sight to make a picture of—that 'twas, comrade.

Well, ne'er saw I such trouble as that

arm gave me (and 't has ne'er been strong since). First 'twould not knit, and then when 't did 'twas all wrong, and had to be broken and set o'er again. But th' lass ne'er gave out once. Late and early, fair weather or foul, a was at th' forge; and a came to be known for as good a smith as there was in all Warwickshire. But, for that none had e'er heard tell o' a woman at such work, or for some other reason, they did come to call her, moreover, " The Farrier Lass o' Piping Pebworth."

One day, as we sat i' th' door o' th' shop, a-resting, and talking together—after a way we had with us even when she was a little lass—there rides up a young gallant, all dressed out in velvet and galloon, and a feather in 's hat, and long curls hanging about his shoulders. Oh ay, a was bonny enough to look upon. So a draws rein at th' door. And saith he,

" Art thou th' Farrier Lass o' Piping Pebworth?" saith he.

10

Saith she, arising to her feet, and standing with crossed arms like any man—saith she,

"Folks call me so," saith she. "But my name is Keren Lemon."

"A sour name for so sweet a lass," saith th' gallant.

"Would thou hadst sweetened that old jest with some new wit!" quoth she.

"Thou art sharp o' tongue," saith he.

"I shoe horses with my arms, not with my tongue," saith she.

"As I live, a witty jade!" quoth he. "Thou dost much amuse me, maiden."

"My wit was not fashioned any more for thy amusement than for the shoeing o' thy horse," quoth she. "So, if thou dost not purpose to have him shod, ride on!" saith she.

Then saith he, to himself, as 'twere, "Verily," saith he, "they should call thee the *harrier* lass, for thou hast run down and found my manners when that old hounds have failed." And to her he saith,

"I do purpose to have my horse shod, maiden; and I cry thee pardon for having given thee offence."

"It is easier to give offence than pardon," saith she. "Howbeit, thou art pardoned. Say no more." Whereupon she sets to work and, taking th' horse's foot atween her knees, falls to filing his hoof in such wise that I could not 'a' done better in her place, though the Queen should ask me to sup afterwards at St. James's. But the stranger could not hold his tongue; and when he saw her working th' bellows, and a-making of th' shoe, and th' way she swung th' great hammer, "By my troth," saith he, "I would I could paint thee as Sally Mander to give to th' Queen," saith he.

Then saith my lass, "I know not of any wench called Sally Mander," saith she, a-burning of th' horse's hoof with th' hot shoe; "but if she consorts familiarly with such as be above her," so saith she, "methinks 'tis as well for both o' us that I know her not," saith she—every word o't just as I tell thee.

Then saith the gallant, clapping hand to thigh, so that it made such a sound as when a young child is trounced, "By my troth," saith he, "an thy brows be not worthy o' a coronet, ne'er saw I any that merited to wear one. What wouldst thou if thou wert a lady, lass?"

She saith, a-rolling up of her sleeves a little tighter, and looking up at him as he sate again upon his horse, "Meanest thou if I were the wife o' a lord?" saith she.

"Even so," saith he, laughing. "Verily thou hast come at my meaning with a commendable quickness. Well, and if thou wert the wife o' a lord, what wouldst thou do?"

Then saith she, speaking very slowly, and crossing of her arms again upon her breast—saith she,

"I would bring up such sons as were

born to me to behave worthily o' their
station in life, and not to forget their manhood by speaking with insolence unto such
honest maids as had never offered them
affront." Whereupon she did up with her
kit o' tools, and pass by me into th' forge;
and th' man rode on with a reddened
visage.

But it befell only two days later that a
came again to th' forge, his horse having
cast another shoe.

And again th' lass sets all to right for
him, he keeping a civil tongue in 's head
this time; and o' that we thought naught
one way or th' other. But when a comes
a third time, and yet a fourth and a fifth
and a sixth, "Father," saith th' lass—"father," saith she, "this must be stopt," saith
she.

"Ay, verily," saith I. "But how wilt do
't?" saith I.

"I'll do 't, never fear," saith she.

And a did, comrade. Ha! ha! I'd trust

that wench to make Satan keep to heel like any well-broke puppy. 'Twas in this way. The next time th' gallant comes riding up (that being th' seventh time in all, ye mind)—well, the next time up comes riding he, and he saith to her, saith he, "I have come to ask thy service yet again, damsel," saith he; "but Merrylegs hath cast another shoe."

Then saith th' lass—ha! ha!—every word as I tell thee, comrade—saith she, "Methinks, my lord, if my work hold no better than that—methinks," saith she, "'twere as well thou went for th' shoeing o' thy horse to Timothy Makeshift, as lives in Marigold Lane," saith she. "For if it come to th' ears o' others how that I will shoe a horse one day, and th' next how that he will cast th' shoe—if it so be known," saith she, "no more custom will I get to keep my father and mother in their old age."

Then doth he leap down from his horse,

and he doffs his hat as though my lass had been any fine lady; and quoth he,

"Well and justly hast thou spoken; and I do stand confessed of my fault. But, maiden, thou wast not born unto th' life thou leadest; and here in thy presence I do ask thy father to bestow upon me thy hand. I am Sir Dagonet Balfour, of Balfour Hall; and if thou art willing I will make thee my lady."

Now, I was struck dumb as though my tongue had jumped forth o' my mouth, and never a blessed thing could I do saving stare, comrade. But that lass o' mine— that lass o' mine, comrade—she stands and looks at him, and never so much as a glint o' red in her face. And saith she, "My lord," saith she, "if that thou meanest what thou hast said, thou hast forgotten thine estate and not remembered mine. Since God hath not made me a lady, methinks it is not in the power o' one o' His creatures so to do. But I do thank thee for seeking to honor me, and wish thee joy when thou shalt take in wedlock some high-born maiden."

Then saith he, "An I wed not thee, ne'er will I be wed. What! dost thou think I can look on in patience and see a woman such as thou following the trade of a far-rier?"

Then saith she, "If Jesus Christ fol-lowed th' trade o' a carpenter," saith she, "sure," saith she, "Keren Lemon can fol-low th' trade o' a farrier," saith she—every blessed word as I tell thee, comrade. And no more would she have to do with him, but got her into th' forge and left him standing there.

Well, thou might 'a' thought that was th' end o't. Not a bit—not a bit, comrade. Th' knight would be a-riding up at all times and in all weather, and somehow 't gets out i' th' village (though not through my lass, I warrant ye) as how he doth in verity seek to espouse my Keren. Well,

o' all th' tirrits and to-do's as e'er you heard
on!

Methought when Mistress Lemon found
out that th' girl had refused th' gallant's
offer th' house would be a tighter fit for us
three than its shell for an unhatched chick.
'Twas worry, worry, worry, from morn till
night, and from night till morn it was worry, worry, worry, till I scarce knew whether
'twould be better to murder my wife and
hang for 't, or leave her alone and live with
her.

"Th' hussy!" quoth she —"th' ungrate-
ful hussy! a ought to be tossed in a blan-
ket," quoth she, "and thou along with her,
thou jack-pudding, thou ravelling!" quoth
she.

"If I be a jack-pudding," saith I, "I ha'
more descendants than most such," saith I.

"Yea," quoth she, "verily," quoth she;
"and all nine o' th' lads be jacks," saith she,
"and th' wench as very a pudding as e'er
fell to pieces for want o' being held togeth-

er," saith she. " Out on ye both! I'm done with ye!"

" For that, God be praised!" saith I, and left ere she could answer.

But one day as I sate i' th' kitchen, a-cosseting o' my lame arm as though 't had been a babe, I hear a sound o' wheels and a clatter o' horses' hoofs; and, lo! there be a chariot pulled up afore the door, with four gray horses a-making play with their trappings, and a coachman, all wig and gilding, a-sitting on th' box. And ere a could move, out steps a fine dame, with her hair all in hillocks, as 'twere, and a paling o' lace round about her head, like as 't had been a flower-garden, and a farthingale to 'a' covered th' big malt-pot with as little to-do as a hen covers an egg. And up comes she to th' door, and her tire-woman a-holding of her robes, and two footmen going before, and in she comes—like as though Riches and Death had a' th' same right to enter a poor man's house without knocking. And saith she to me, saith she, a-filling up o' the room with her finery, like a cuckoo ruffling out its feathers in another bird's nest, saith she,

" Be this th' cottage o' Humfrey Lemon th' farrier ?" saith she.

" It be so; and I be he," saith **I.**

" And be thou th' father o' th' wench they call th' Farrier Lass o' Piping Pebworth ?" saith she.

" I be, an' proud o't," say I, a-beginning to think that she might 'a' knocked at th' door, for all her greatness.

" Where's th' lass ?" saith she, as she might 'a' said " Where's my glove ?"

Then saith I, " Madam," saith I, "most like she's gone about her business," saith I.

" My good man," saith she, after a fashion that did cause me to feel aught but good — " my good man," saith she, " dost thou know to whom thou speakest ?"

" Verily," saith I, " thou art ahead o' me there, madam."

"Boor," saith she, "I am the Lady o' Balfour Hall."

"An' so could my lass 'a' been, had she willed it," saith I; but ere I could further forget myself, in comes Keren by another door, and she saith,

"Father, do thou go out, and leave me to speak with this lady." Then to th' dame she saith, "Your ladyship," saith she, "I am Keren Lemon, that be called th' Farrier Lass. What wouldst thou with me?"

Then I got me out o' th' room, but not out o' hearing distance; and this is what followed:

"I have heard," saith th' dame, "these reports concerning my son Sir Dagonet and thee, and, to my sorrow, I find upon inquiry," saith she, "that they be true. Moreover, though it doth shame me to the dust to confess it, I have had an interview with my son Sir Dagonet," so saith she—every word o't as I tell thee—"and

he is determined in his purpose o' ruining
his life and th' happiness o' his mother.
Therefore I have come to thee, to ask
that thou persistest in the course which
thou hast begun," saith she. "And here,"
saith she, "is gold to hold thy tongue concerning my visit unto thee." And therewith she did count down ten broad gold
pieces upon th' kitchen table. "I must
also ask thee," then continued she, ere my
lass could answer her, "to allow me to remain under thy roof until my carriage be
returned from th' other end o' the village,
where it hath been sent with my tire-woman to purchase some ribbon to tie my
parrot to 's perch."

Never a word saith my lass, but she goes
to th' door and opens it, and lifting up her
voice, she halloos to a little ragged urchin
who is at some spot on th' other side o' th'
street; and he being come as fast as his
little shanks would bring him, she bids him
enter, and taking him up in her arms, she

lifts him up so that a can reach th' gold on th' table, and saith she,

"Thou'rt not o'er-clean to touch, my good little mouse," saith she, "but thou'rt cleaner than that stuff thou seest. There, lad, that's for thee, if an thou'lt run to th' other end o' th' village and bid them return at once with my lady Balfour's carriage," so saith she. Then, th' lad having stuffed all 's doublet with th' gold, she sets him on 's feet, and off a scuttles on th' best-paid errand e'er chanced since th' world began. And my lass, having courtesied to the thunder-stricken dame, gets her outside (where I go nigh to smothering her with kisses), and leaves her ladyship in possession o' th' kitchen.

Well, comrade, right sure am I that thou dost think that was the end on 't. Not a bit. Sir Dagonet did himself come to th' cottage th' very next day to see th' lass, and they had many words together, and at last he did accuse her o' false pride and proud humility. And saith he,

"Wouldst thou make misery for the man who loves thee best of all the world, merely to satisfy a notion o' thine own? Greatness and goodness," saith he, "dwell in the heads and hearts o' mankind, not in their birth or purses. I do ask thee, with all respect, to be my wife, and I am prepared to face th' anger o' my mother and o' th' Queen. Ay," saith he, his face gone red as a girl's, and comes nigh to her—"ay, maiden," saith he, "I am even ready to seek th' new country with thee as my wife, and to leave title and lands and Queen and mother behind me."

Then saith she—and I had not seen tears in her eyes for many a day—

"My lord," saith she, "well and nobly hast thou spoken, and with all my soul do I honor thee for it, and I thank thee with all my heart and soul. But, my lord, even were there not thy rank and position atween us, there is atween us," saith she, " which would hold us as far apart as the sea doth hold this England which we live in and th' new country o' which thou didst speak. For," saith she — and she speaks in a steady voice, howbeit 'tis very low, and she keeps her sun-like eyes on his— " for, my lord," saith she, " all the love that was mine to give hath been another man's these many years."

Then saith he never another word, but bends his knee and kisses her long brown hand as though 't had been th' Queen's; and he gets him from th' cottage.

Now, two more years were sped since that Ruth had left us, and sometimes would we hear through friends o' th' little lad and 's mother and father, and always was Ruth a-sending of pretty messages to Keren—her love, and her thanks, and how happy she was, and th' boy so like his father—and more than I remember.

A full year had th' lass been at work in

my shop, and my arm no more fit to hammer than afore. So I looks about to get
a lad to help her in her work, seeing as
'twere too much for one wench. And,
Lord! th' trouble I had! Ten lads did I
try, one right after th' other; and one
would be saucy, and another dull, and another would take 't into his pumpkin head
to fall in love wi' th' lass; and all o' 'em
lazy. But, God-a-mercy! how's a man to
tell a lazy lad till he ha' tried him?—unless
it be old Butter. Ha! ha! I ha' just
minded me o' th' way he used to treat th'
lads that came to Amhurste to hire for un-
der-gardeners. He would stand with 's
owlish old visage a-set on 's hoe-handle, for
all th' world like a fantastic head carved
out o' a turnip and set on a stick, and a
would let th' lad go on with 's story o' how
Dame This commended him for that, and
o' how Dame That commended him for
this, and o' how a had worked under my
lord So-and-So's head-gardener and in my

11

lady So-and-So's own hot-houses; and
when a had got through, never a word
would old Butter say, but a would just step
round behind th' lad, as solemn as a grave-
digger on a cold day, and a would lift up
th' tail o' 's doublet and look at th' seat o'
's breeches. And if they were fairly worn
a would hire th' lad; but if an they were
much worn a would say, " No work dost
thou get from me, my lad," would a say,
"thou sittest down too often to work for
Anthony Butter"—so would a say—every
word o't just as I ha' told thee. Ha! ha!
And all the time as sober as a coroner
inspecting a corse. Ha! ha! ha! Methinks I can see him now—th' old zany.

Well, well, a was a good man, was Anthony Butter; and if a was a bit puffed up
with 's own importance, a's charity ne'er
got in a like condition that it did not bring
forth some kind act.

Well, th' months swung round, and 'twas
nigh to Martlemas in that same year, and

one day as I sat i' th' forge door, a-swearing roundly to myself concerning my lame arm, and how that 'twould not mend, up comes galloping a man, like one distraught, and a child on th' saddle afore him, and a flings himself down with th' child in 's arms (making no shift whate'er to hold th' horse, which gallops on with th' reins swinging), and a cries out, a-setting of th' child on my knee—a cries out,

"For God's sake, help me! My child hath been bit by a mad dog! Help me in some way, for th' love of God!"

And I saw that 'twas Robert Hacket that crouched and quivered at my knee like a hurt hound, and th' child as like to him as one leaf on a tree is to th' other. But ere I could do or say aught, comes that lass o' mine, and ups with th' babe in her arms, and he roaring as lustily as any bull-calf with th' wound in 's little brown arm, and she sees where the beast hath bitten him. Then sets she him down

again on my lap, and runs and fetches a
bar o' iron and heats it i' th' forge till 'tis
white-hot, and all th' time th' poor father
a-sobbing, and kissing of th' babe, and calling on me to help him, like as though I
were God Almighty. And while he was
so doing, and the babe like to burst with
weeping, and I gone mad with not knowing what to be at, comes that wench, comrade, and jerks up th' babe, and sets th'
white-hot metal in 's soft flesh.

Ay, comrade, a did, and a held it there
till where th' dog's fangs had been was
burned as black as th' anvil. And then,
when 'tis done, and th' babe again upon 's
feet, and we two for praising and blessing
o' her, down drops she all in a heap on th'
floor atween us, like a hawk that hath been
smitten in mid-heaven. Then 'twas, comrade, that th' babe was left to endure his
pain as best he might; never thought more
did 's father give him that day; but he
runs and lifts th' lass in 's strong arms, and

bears her out into th' fresh air, and he calls her his "dear," and his "own," and "his life," and his " Keren," till, had 't not been for my lass's coming back to life, I would 'a' struck him on th' mouth for a-speaking so unto her, and he th' husband o' another woman.

But no sooner opes she her eyes than he hath both her hands hid in one o' his, and close against his breast, and she lying back in 's arms as though she were any chrisom child, and her big eyes wide on his, and he saith to her,

" Lass! lass!" saith he, " I ha' come to marry thee, an thou wilt have me," quoth he. " I ha' come to marry thee; and may God bless thee for saving th' child!"

Then did I understand; but she saith, with her great eyes not moving—saith she —only one word—" Ruth ?" saith she, even so, once, low like that—" Ruth ?"

" Ay, lass, I know," he saith unto her. " I know," he saith. " But all's well with Ruth. Ruth is in heaven."

Then saith she, while a light leaps out o' her tearful eyes, like as when the sun doth shine suddenly through April rain — saith she, as she were breathing her life into th' words,

"Methinks I be there too."

And also did I understand her, how that she meant that to be lying in th' arms o' him she loved, after all those weary years, was like being in heaven; but he questions her.

"How, lass?" saith he. "Where dost thou think thou art? Thou art in thy true love's arms," saith he.

"Ay, there is heaven," she saith.

And I stole away to get th' babe some kickshaws i'. th' village, that they twain might be alone together.

Well, well, all that was two year ago, comrade—two year ago; and now that lass o' mine hath a babe o' her own, and as valiant a rogue as ever bellowed. Thou must come and sup with us to-night. Na, na, I'll

take no refusal — dost hear? I will not.
And a word o' persuasion i' thy ear, comrade: Mistress Lemon hath been dead
this twelvemonth, comrade. Ah ha! Wilt
a-come the now? That's well. And thou
shalt hear that lass o' mine troll thee " Jog
on, jog on," and " Mistress mine, where art
thou roaming?" and " Listen, Robin, while
I woo." Come, comrade, come. But stay;
let's crack another drink together ere we
go. Joel! What there! Joel, I say! Another quart o' sack for Master Turnip!

NURSE CRUMPET TELLS THE STORY.

Time.— A bitter January night in the year of Grace
1669.

Scene.—Sunderidge Castle—The great hall—A monstrous fire burning in the big fireplace — Nurse
Crumpet discovered seated on a settle — At her
either knee lean the little Lady Dorothy and her
brother, the young Earl of Sunderidge, Lord Humphrey Lennox.

Nurse Crumpet.—Nay, now, Lady Dorothy, why wilt thou be at the pains o' such
a clamoring?   Sure thou hast heard that
old tale o'er a hundred times; and thou
too, my lord?   Fie, then!   Wouldst seek
to flatter thy old nurse with this seeming
eagerness?   Go to!   I say thou canst not
in truth want to hear me drone o'er that
ancient narrative.   Well, then, an I must,

I must. Soft! Hold my fan betwixt thy
dainty cheeks and the blaze, sweetheart,
lest the fire-fiend witch thy roses into very
poppy flowers. And thou, my lord, come
closer to my side, lest the draught from the
bay-window smite thee that thou howlest o'
th' morrow with a crick i' thy neck. Well,
well, be patient. All in time, in time. Soft,
now! Ye both mind that I was but a little lass when thy grandmother, the Lady
Elizabeth Lennox, did take me to train as
her maid-in-waiting. I was just turned six-
teen that Martlemas, and not a fair-sized
wench for my years either. Would ye believe? I could set my two thumbs together at my backbone in those days, and my
ring-fingers would all but kiss too.

Lord Humphrey.—Ha! ha! Nurse, thy
fingers would be but ill satisfied lovers under those conditions nowadays. Eh, Dolly?

Lady Dorothy.—Hold thy tongue for an
unmannerly lad, Humphrey. Do not thou
heed him, nurse, but go on with thy story.

Nurse Crumpet.—For all thy laughter, my lord, I'd a waist my garter would bind in those days, and was as light on my toes as those flames that dance i' th' chimney. Lord! Lord! how well I mind me o' th' first time that e'er I clapt eyes on Jock Crumpet! I was speeding home with a jug o' water from the spring, and what with his staring as he stood at the road-side to let me pass, and what with a root i' th' way, I all but lost my footing. Yet did I swing round alone, holding fast my jug, and ne'er one blessed drop o' water spilled I, for all my tripping. "By'r lay'kin!" quoth he, "thou'rt as light on thy feet as a May wind, and as I live I will dance the Barley Break with thee this harvesting or I will dance with none!" And i' faith a was as good as his word, for by hook or by crook, and much scheming and planning, and bringing o' gewgaws to my mother, and a present o' a fine yearling to my father, that harvesting did I dance the Barley Break

with Jock Crumpet. And a was a feather-
man in a round reel.

Well, 'twas the year o' my meeting with
Jock, thou mindst. (And a cold winter
that was—Christ save us! There be ne'er
such winters nowadays. This night is as
a summer noon i' th' comparison.) 'Twas
the year o' my first meeting with Jock, and
my lady, your grandmother, sent for me to
the castle, to be her waiting-maid. Lord!
'twas a troublous time! What with joy at
my good fortune, and sorrow at quitting
my mother, I was fain to smile with one
corner o' my mouth and look grievously
with the other, like a zany at a village fair.
And Jock, he would not that I went, for
that he could not see me, or consort wi'
me so often: Jock was aye honey-combed
wi' th' thing ye call "sentiment." A would
grin on a flower I had wov'n in my locks
by th' hour together. And 'tis my belief
a could a spun him a warm doublet out
o' the odds and ends o' ribbon and what

not he had filched from me when my eyes
were elsewhere. And Jock — but 'tis neither here nor there o' Jock. In those days
thy grandmother had only one child, a little lass, the Lady Patience. And ne'er was
man or maid worse named; for to call such
a flibbertigibbet " Patience " were as though
one should name a frisksome colt "Slum-
ber," or christen a spring brook " Quiet."
Patience, quotha! 'Twas patience in truth
a body had need of, who was thrown at all
with her little ladyship. But there was
ne'er so beautiful a maiden born in all the
broad land of England; nor will be again
—not though London Tower be standing
when the last trump sounds. Meseemed
she was an elf-sprite, so tiny was she; and
her face like a fair flower, so fresh and
pure. Her hair was shed about her face
like sunlight on thistle-down, and her eyes
made a shining behind it, like the big blue
gems in her mother's jewel-box. When
she laughed, it was as water falling into

water from a short height, with ripples, and
little murmurs, and a clear tinkling sound.
But she was ne'er more at rest than the
leaves on an aspen-tree. Hither and thither would she flit, this way and that, up and
down, round and round, backward and forward, about and about. I' faith, ofttimes
would I be right dizzy come nightfall, with
following of her; for ere I had been at the
castle a day, she took so mighty a fancy
to me, that naught would do but she must
have me for her maid; and so my lady,
who (God pardon my boldness!) did utter-
ly spoil her in all things, gave me unto her
as a nurse-maid.—But sure ye are a-weary
o' this old tale!

*Lady Dorothy and Lord Humphrey in a
breath.*—Nay, go on, go on.

Nurse Crumpet.—Well, well, o' all the
story - loving bairns! But I must invent
me a new history for the next time o' telling.

Lord Humphrey.— Nay, that thou shalt

not. We will ne'er like any as well as we like this one. So despatch.

Nurse Crumpet.—But my lady had also an adopted daughter, a niece o' my lord's —one Mistress Marian Every — and she walked beside the little Lady Patience as night might walk beside day, for she was as brown o' skin as a mountain stream, and her hair like a cloud at even - tide, dark, but of no certain color, albeit as soft as rav-elled silk, and marvellous hard to comb on account o' its fineness. Mistress Marian was full head and shoulders taller than her cousin, the Lady Patience, and she could lift her aloft in her arms, and swing her from side to side, as a supple bough swings a bird. And her eyes were dark, and cool to gaze into, like a pool o' clear water o'er autumn leaves, and sometimes there were glints o' light in them, like the spikes i' th' evening-star when thou dost gaze steadily upon it. Black and white were not more different than were they, and they resembled even less in mind than they did in body. When Lady Patience waxed wroth, her cheeks burned like two coals, and thou couldst hear her little teeth grinding together, like pebbles squeezed i' th' palm o' thy hand; but when Mistress Marian was an-angered, the blood rushed back to her heart, and she was whiter than a lamb at the shearing, and her lips like white threads. Then would the light shoot and spin in her eyes, and her nostrils suck in and out, like those of a fretful horse. And she was fierce after the manner of a man rather than of a maid. Moreo'er, she was full a year younger than the Lady Patience; but she looked it not; rather did her ladyship look full two years younger than Mistress Marian. And I loved them both, and tried as a Christian not to prefer one before the other; but what with my lady's stealings of her arms about my neck as I sat at my stitchery, and popping of comfits in my pocket when I would be otherwise engaged, and teasings, and ticklings, and sundry other pretty witcheries which I do not at this day recall, I was fairly cozened into loving her the best. (Honey, I charge thee hold my fan betwixt thee and the fire.) But to continue. —Mistress Marian was aye courteous and kindly to me as heart could wish, and every night did she thank me i' th' prettiest fashion, when I had combed and unpinned her for the night; but, Lord! I had much ado to get Lady Patience combed or unpinned at all! First would she jump with both knees upon mine, and hug my very breath away; then, when I had at last coaxed her to get down, first she would perch on one leg and then o' the other, and then be a-twisting her head now over this shoulder, now over that, to see how I came on with the unpinning, that it was with a prayer to God that I finally set her night-gown over her shoulders, and led her to bed. As for her prayers

—Jesu aid me and pardon her!—'twas a
matter of hours to get her to say " Our
Father" straight through, what with her
vowing that she wished not bread every
day, and how that if his lordship her father
forgave not trespassers (for I could ne'er
draw the difference between trespass*es* and
trespass*ers* into her pretty pate), neither
would she; and how she did not believe
God would lead her into temptation at any
time, but that it was the Devil; and how
it must anger God even to think of such
doings on His part—what, I say, with all
this, methought sometimes it would be cock-
crow ere I got her safely to sleep. And
all this time Mistress Marian would be lying
as quiet as any mouse, with her big plait of
hair between her fingers, for so she always
slept, with her hair fast in her hands, as
though she loved its beauty; and in truth it
was the one great beauty she had, for my
little lady put her out with her glitter as the
sunlight doth extinguish a morning moon.

Now I had been at the castle scarce two months when one day it chances that I hear my lady a-telling o' my lord how as her brother, Lord Charles Radnor, dying wifeless, had left his only son to her care until he should come of age. And on that Tuesday the little lord set foot in the castle; and my lady was down at the door-way to meet him, in a new velvet gown, with her wimple sewn in fine pearls, and my lord with her; but my two nurslings waxed shy at the last minute, and would not come down, but leaned and peered through the posts o' the stair-rail, and my little lady let fall one o' her shoes in her eagerness to glimpse at her new cousin. And straightway ran the lad and lifted the wee shoe, and looked upward, laughing, and my lord and lady having retired into the dining-hall, to see that some cold viands were in readiness (it being then near to nightfall, though not yet supper hour).— "Ho! thou little cinder witch," cried he;

"I am the prince that has found thy shoe, and when I shall have found thee, if that thy temper be as small as thy shoe, fear not but that I will kiss thee too!" With that, he ran up the stair-way, two and three steps at a leap.

And I followed, for I knew not what would happen an he claimed his kiss as he had threatened (knowing as did I, that in verity my lady's shoe would a been a tight fit for her temper).

But when he was arrived at the top, lo! they had both fled, neither had they left so much as a ribbon behind them. Then the lad laughed again, as pleasant a laugh as e'er I heard in all my days, and quoth he, "I would be but a poor prince an I had not to search for my little princess." So off he starts, and I after him, up and down corridors, in at half-open doors, out upon balconies, hither and thither, after the manner o' my little lady on her most unquiet days, till at last, for the sake o' peace,

I did slyly lead him in the direction o' the great nursery. There, catching sight o' a little red petticoat, he enters, where stand my truant elves confessed, Mistress Marian frowning and biting o' her dark hair, but my little lady like to stifle, with both hands over her mouth to hide her smiles, and her blue eyes dancing a very Barley Break o' mirth among the yellow sheaves o' her tresses.

Then there was much parley o'er the fitting o' the shoe, as both damsels did straightway sit down upon their feet, neither for a long time would they move an eyelash, till his lordship, with a twink o' his eye at me, did suggest corns and bunions as a reason for their 'havior — and, Lord! then 'twas pretty to mark how like little chicks beneath their dam's feathers, first one little foot and then the other did steal out from the rich lace o' their petticoats. And ere one could cry " Oh !" for a pinch, he had slipt the shoe on my little lady's wee foot, and had kissed her right heartily. Moreo'er, what I did most marvel at, was that she neither cuffed nor sought to cuff him, but dropt down her head until her hair made a veil before her face, and moved that foot whereon he had set her shoe, gently back and forth as though the leather was stiff to her ankle, and I saw that she looked at it from under her heavy hair. But Mistress Marian still held aloof, and chewed upon her dark locks like a heifer on its cud. And her eyes were every whit as dark and solemn as a very cow's. Then the young lord laughed again, and cried out, " Ha ! the ox - eyed June !" or some such apery, and went and kneeled before her in mock fashion, as before a queen, and quoth he, " Fair goddess " (for 'twas afterwards explained to me what manner of being was a goddess, namely, some kind of a foreign fairy)— " Fair goddess," quoth he, " show me how I may dispel thy wrath." And still she scowled on him, but spoke no word. And he continued, and said, " I prithee, fair lady, cast but one smile upon thy humble knight" (thou mind'st their pretty foolery has stuck i' my old pate unto this day).

Then she answered and saith, "Thou silly lad, how can I be a goddess and a lady both in one? Thou hast not even enough wit to make a good fool. So!" (for Mistress Marian had a sharp tongue at times).

But he was not so much as ruffled, and laughed even again, most heartily. And he said, " I do perceive that thou art not fashioned either as goddess or lady, therefore be my comrade, and we will fight together for the weal o' yon fairy princess." All at once she laughed too, and yielded him her hand, and said, " I like thee. What is thy name?"

He said, " My name is Ernle; and I like thee too; therefore, I pray thee, tell me thine."

So she told him, and my little lady sidling up, the three fell presently a-chattering like linnets at sunrise, and from that hour on I had no trouble with them.

'Twas pretty to mark them at their fantasies. They were aye out-o'-door save when 'twas rainy weather, and then methought the castle had scarce room enough for them. In all their games Mistress Marian was the little lord's comrade, and wore a helmet o' silvered wood, and carried a wooden sword silvered to match her head-gear, and the little lord was likewise apparelled. And he called her ever " Comrade," and clapped her o' th' shoulder, as mankind will clap one the other when conversing.

But my little lady, they both agreed, was a fairy princess; and, Lord, Lord! 'twould take me from now 'til Martlemas next to name the perilous 'scapes that did befall her. They fished her out of moats, they bore her from blazing castles, they did drag her from the maws o' dragons and other wild beasts I know not how to name. Thrice was the little Lord of Radnor in dire straits at the claws o' goblin creatures. Three times did his comrade rescue him by thwacking upon the chair which did represent the dreadful beast, till I was in sore dread there would be no mending of it, and me, mayhap, dismissed from the castle for carelessness. And always when 'twas all o'er, and the little princess in safety, I was called upon to act parson and wed my little lady to the little lord, while Mistress Marian leaned on her sword to witness the doings.

One day, in their rovings through the park, they came by chance upon a door in the hill-side, but so o'ergrown with creeping vines that, had not the little lord stumbled upon it, 'twas very like it had been there to this day without discovery. Well, no sooner do they see the door than they must needs open it, spite o' all my scolding, and peer within. 'Twas but a darksome hole, after all—a kind o' cave i' th' hill-side, which they did afterwards find out from thy grandfather was used in days gone by for con-

cealing treasures in time of war. And indeed it seemed a safe place, for there were
two rusty bolts as big as my arm, one o' th'
inside and one o' th' outside, and the creeping things hid all. As thou mightst think,
it grew to be their favorite coigne for play-
ing their dragon and princess trickeries. I
would sit with my stitchery on a fallen log
in the sunshine, while they ran in and out
o' th' grewsome hole. But in all their frol-
icking my little lady could ne'er abide the
sight o' their swords, and she pleaded ever
for gentler games. One day (I shall ne'er
forget, though I live to see doomsday) they
did crown her a queen, and then my lord
would have it that she dubbed him her
knight. She pleaded that prettily against
it methought the veriest boor in Christen-
dom would a given in to her, but my little
lord was stanch. So they made her a
throne o' flowers, and when she was seated
thereon, Mistress Marian handed her the
great wooden sword, and my lord, kneeling,

bade her strike him on the shoulder with the flat side o' th' sword, saying, " Rise, Sir Ernle, my knight for evermore !"

She got out the words as he bade her, but when 't came to the stroke, what with her natural fright, and what with the sunlight on the silver, she brought down the heavy blade edgewise on the boy's pate, laying wide quite a gash above his left eyebrow, so that the blood trickled down his cheek. When she saw that, meseemed all the blood in her body went to keep his company, for she turned whiter than her smock, and ran and got her arm about him and saith, o'er and o'er again, " Ernle ! Ernle ! I have killed thee !"

He laughed, to comfort her, and made light of it, and wetting his finger in the blood, drew a cross on his brow and said, " Nay, thou hast not killed me. And more-o'er, I am not only thy knight, but thy Red Cross Knight into the bargain, and thou my lady forever. See ! I will seal thee with my

very blood!" and ere she could draw back,
he had set also a cross on her white brow.
She shuddered and fell a-weeping, and drew
her hand across her brow to wipe away the
ugly stain; and when she saw that she had
but smeared it on her hand, she trembled
more than ever, and it was not for some
days that I could quiet her.

I do but relate this story, to show in what
horror my little lady did ever hold swords
and bloodshed.

Well, to continue—

This could not last for aye, and when two
more years were sped, his uncle sent the
little lord to a place o' learning; and afterwards to travel to and fro upon the earth,
after the manner of Satan in the Book of
Job (God forgive me! but 't has ever seemed like that to me). And we set not eyes
on him for eight years. Now in that time,
lo! I was married, and my little lady and
Mistres Marian in long kirtles, and their
hair looped up upon their heads. Mistress

Marian was yet full head and shoulders above my little lady, and her skin as brown as ever. But my little lady was as bright and slender as a sun-ray.

They would speak to me sometimes of Lord Radnor, and how that great folks were saying great things of him, and how he was become a soldier and a marvellous person altogether; but as the years went by they seemed not so ready to talk o' him, only sometimes my little lady would pull down my head as I smoothed the bed-clothes over her at night, and quoth she, "Nurse, dost think he will be much changed? My hair hath not darkened much, hath it? Dost think his curls will be different from what they were when he was a lad?" And I would have to tell her "No" a dozen times ere she would let me go. But Mistress Marian said never a word.

One day I learned of my lady how that Lord Radnor was to return the next week, and meseemed in truth the whole castle was waxed distraught.

It is not in my power to tell o' th' doings, but suffice it to say, my lord did cozen them all, and come a full day ere he was expected.

When he came, Mistress Marian was standing i' th' great door o' th' castle, in her hawking gown o' green velure cloth laced all with silver cord; her plumed hat was on her curls, and her hawk, Beryl, on her fist. And she turned and beheld him. Ne'er did I see verier light in earth or sky, than flashed into her face as their eyes met. And he doffed his hat, and came up beside her on the step, and saith, with the old laugh, but gentler, " Well met, comrade."

Now when he called her " comrade," 'twas as when Jock did call me " sweetheart" in the days o' our wooing. She went red as the ribbon in his sleeves; and when the falcon fretted and shook its bells, he did put out his hand and stroke it, and, lo! it was still, and seemed to feel him as its master. And I wondered all this time where could be my little lady.

To this day I have ne'er seen so handsome a man as the young lord. He was tall and straight as an oak, with curls the color of frost-touched oak-leaves i' th' sunlight, and eyes like the amber drink when men hold it aloft ere quaffing, and his whole countenance bright and eager, and narrow like that o' a fox, but without a fox's cunning. Then he seemed fashioned to run, and ride, and war, as doth become all men, whether of high or low estate.

Then went I within to inquire after my little lady; and Jock, who was become a footman i' th' castle, did tell me of how he had seen her set forth to walk i' th' park an hour gone. So straightway I went in search of her.

I had gone some six hundred paces when, at a sudden turning, I came upon her, where she held a little urchin a-strad-

dle of her big deer-hound "Courage." The
child gave chuckles o' delight as he slipped
from side to side, and the sun through the
beech-leaves made their heads as like as
two crown pieces. Even as I was about to
lift up my voice to halloo unto her, lo! my
lord doth part the thick branches, and steps
forth a little behind her, and stands watch-
ing her. And as he did stand there, behold, a look came o'er his face, that was
stranger than any look I had e'er seen on
th' face of man or of woman, and his eyes
were no more bright and eager, but deep
and soft. Then she turned and went direct
towards him unknowing.

When she was beside him, still laughing and half out o' breath with balancing
o' th' heavy boy, he saith these two words,
"My lady," and methought there was a
whole year's love - making o' ordinary men
crammed into them. Quoth I to myself:
"Ah, my little lord, so thou hast that trick
with thee! God keep my little ladies! for

if the tongue be a fire, how must it burn when such a wit doth wag it!" And I determined in my heart that by some means I would warn my little lady of his sweet speecheries. Yet was I tender towards him for the sake o' by-gone days. Mayhap, moreover, his comely face had something to do with it, for, i' fecks, ne'er saw I a goodlier countenance on Roundhead or Cavalier.

Now when my lady heard his voice at her ear, first gives she such a start as doth a mettlesome filly when a hare jumps out before it, then stock-still stands she, and her face whiter than a wind-flower, and her lips a-tremble as if to speak, but no word comes from them.

He saith again, " My lady."

I saw by the moving of her lips that she fashioned the words "My God!" but still she spoke not. And the child began to whimper and clutch at her kirtle, for she had loosened her hold of him, and he feared falling off of the big dog. So she put one arm about him to hold him, but her eyes were yet upon his lordship.

Then he came and lifted her hand to his breast, and it lay upon his dark-green doublet, as a white flower-leaf doth upon grass, and he saith to her, " Sweetheart, dost thou not know me ?"

All at once, for what, God only knoweth, she fell a-weeping, and he had her in his arms. And being some two years a mother, my care was all for the poor little rogue on the deer-hound; 'twas as much as I could do to hold back from running and snatching him in my arms to soothe his terror.

Howbeit, ere that I could commit this madness, the frighted babe set up such a howl as only a man-child can utter, and my lady turned to him in great haste, and my lord also did set about comforting him. Then they walked slowly on, and my lord held the little lad on one side, and my lady coaxed him o' th' other. Ever and anon

13

my lord would look from the babe to my lady, and then from my lady to the babe. And a smile just lifted the corners o' his mouth, as sometimes a wind will just stir the leaves ere shaking them as with jollity. I followed cautiously at some distance, and by-and-by his lordship said, " How was it that thou didst not know me, coz?   Faith thou art shot up like a lily i' th' sun, but lilies are aye lilies, and leaving thee a lily, I find thee a lily still, though blooming on a taller stem."

And she answered him: "Yea, cousin, and oaks are aye oaks, though first they be saplings, then trees.   And in truth I knew thee by thy voice ere I looked at thee; but 'twas all so sudden, that i' faith I was frightened at thee."

And he said, " But thou art glad to see me?"

And being busy with the child, she answered him without lifting her head, " Thou knowest that I am."

Then did he laugh a little, and saith, "How should I know, coz? Proof, proof, I pray thee. Wilt thou not give me the kiss o' welcome after all these years?"

Now he had not offered to kiss Mistress Marian. Therefore I waited right curiously to see what my little lady would say unto his offer, and Jock having dinned it into my ears ever since our wedding-day, that all women were by nature eavesdroppers, I was of a mind to prove his theory for him; so I not only listened with all my ears, but I looked with all my eyes.

My lady waxed first ruddy, then like to milk, then ruddy again, and she reached out her hand to him across the hound. "In truth I will, cousin," quoth she.

He did take the little hand in his, putting down his other hand softly over it, as when one holds a frighted bird, and he looked at her as though he would pierce her lids with his gaze, for her eyes were down, and he saith, "Sweetheart, right

gladly will I give this pretty hand the kiss
o' an eternal welcome; but methinks thou
hast begged the question. I pleaded to re-
ceive a kiss rather than to bestow one."

And her face was like a bended rose.
Then did he step round quickly beside her,
and once more was the poor babe left in
dire terror o' his life, and he made up a
piteous face, but the dog standing still, he
fell to rattling its collar, and soon waxed
merry with the jingle o' th' silver. So I
looked again at my lady and Lord Radnor.

He had taken her about her waist with
one arm, and with the other hand he lifted
gently upward her fair face, as doth a gardener a rain-beaten flower, while his eyes
looked down into hers. And slowly, slowly, almost as rose-leaves unfurl i' th' sun,
her white lids curled upward, and her blue
eyes peered softly from her yellow locks
like corn-flowers through ripe corn, there
being a tear in each, as when a rain-bead
doth tremble i' th' real corn-flowers. And,

to be the more like nature, there ran big waves throughout her loosened tresses, like as when the wind doth steal across a field o' grain on summer noons.

Then he bended down his tall head, and their lips met. God alone knows what their first words would a been, for ere the kiss was well ended, down falls the poor little rogue off of the hound's back, and lifts up his voice loud enow to be heard across the sea by the red men i' the new continent. And my lady runs and lifts him in her arms. Lord! such an ado as they had a-comforting him! First my lady, then my lord, then my lady again — and at last my lord tosses him to his shoulder, and saith he,

"Ho! thou little Jack Pudding! an thou art not still o' th' instant, I'll swear thou art a girl, an' thou shalt ne'er have a sword such as men have."

And as I live, the child stinted, and waxed as solemn as an owl! Not another tear did he shed. My lord saith,

"Now thou art a good lad, therefore thou shalt have my sword to play with." And he unbinds it from his side, scabbard and all, and holds it while the urchin gets astride o't and pretends to ride. When my lord is tired o' stooping, he lifts the child again to his shoulder, and so do they conduct him back to his mother, the gardener's wife. From thence they return to the castle, and are met by my lord and lady and all the servants, while I haste me in by a side door to get on my Sunday kirtle and appear with the rest.

As time wore on, the three were as much together as when he was a little lad and they lassies, and sometimes from a window, and sometimes from a quiet coigne in the great hall (this very hall, ye mind, dears), I would sit with my stitchery and mark them at their bright chatter.

But often Mistress Marian would come and sit against my knee, even as thou art sitting now, sweetheart, and ask me to stroke her hair, and when she would coax Lord Ernle's big blood-hound "Valor" to come and lie beside her, she would sit more quiet, almost as though she were asleep. And she would ask me ever and again, "Nurse, wherefore are women at any time born with dark hair, to mar ev'n such small comeliness as they might otherwise have?"

And always I would answer, "Tut! thou knowest not of what thou speakest, my honey; in the sight o' some, dark hair is more comely than fair hair." And always she would shake her head, and smile i' th' fashion o' one who knows better than another. But she was a wondrous fair woman, in spite o' her own thinking, and shaped like the brown metal wench over yonder with the bow and arrows. Diana, say ye? Why, even so; so it was that his lordship called her when he did not call her "comrade."

Now young Sir Rowland Nasmyth (him who was father to that Sir Rowland who

wedded your sister the Lady Anne last
Michaelmas, ye mind, dears), he would be
often over for a day, or maybe several
days, at the castle; and all four would ride
a-hawking, or ramble together, two by two,
through the park; or Lord Ernle and Sir
Rowland would play at rackets, and i' fecks
'twas a sight to see 'em at it! One day my
little lady and Sir Rowland (who was a fair
stripling, with curls near the color o' Mistress Marian's, and eyes the tinting o' the
far sea on a rainy day) did wander off together, and Mistress Marian and my lord
were left alone, seated on a rude bench under one o' th' great beech-trees that flank
the hall door. He leaned forward and rested
an elbow on either knee, and did let his
racket swing back and forth between them,
and sat looking down on it. Mistress Marian's gaze was upon him, but her big hat
made so deep a shadow o'er her eyes withal
that I could not note them clearly. So
stayed they for some moments.

Then all in a breath did Lord Ernle start erect and push back his heavy locks and speak. "Comrade," saith he, "wilt thou call me an ass for my pains, I wonder, an I tell thee o' something that is troubling me sorely?"

She, having in no wise moved from her first position, and her eyes still in shadow, saith, "I pray thee say on, Ernle, for such words as thou hast just spoken to me are idle."

And he leaned forward and took one of her long brown hands in his, but 'twas different from the way in which he had ta'en my little lady's hand at their first meeting, and he saith, "Comrade, for thou hast e'er been my true and loyal comrade, Marian— sweet comrade-cousin — this is the matter that doth eat my heart. Dost think there is aught between Patience and that young coxcomb?"

There came a red mark all across her brow, as though he had smitten her, for

with her sudden movement her hat had
fallen upon the ground at her feet.   And
she put up her hand to her side as if in
pain, but snatched it back quickly.   And
for one heart-beat she shut her eyes.   My
lord, who had stooped forward to lift her
hat, saw none o' this, and when the hat was
again upon her brow and its shadow over
her face, she seemed the same as ever.
But I knew the shaft was in her heart, and
my heart seemed to feel it, for I loved her
dearly.   When he could wait no longer, he
said, " Well, comrade ?"

And she spoke, for from the hair that
crowned her to the feet that carried her
she was as brave as any Cavalier that ever
swung sword for the King, and she said,
" Well indeed, cousin, for thee."

He said, " How dost thou mean for
me ?"

Then stooped she and gathered a hand-
ful of grass, and held it aloft and opened
her hand, palm downward, that the falling

blades were blown this way and that by the wind.

"I mean," quoth she, "that Rowland Nasmyth is no more to Patience than—I am to thee." And she laughed a little.

He came closer to her, and laid his arm about her shoulders, drawing her to him, and he said, "Nay, thou knowest how dear thou art to me, comrade; but thou meanest in different wise—is't so?"

She said, "Yea; but call me Marian to-day. It is to my whim."

He answered, "Dear Marian," and would have kissed her cheek, but she started up with a little cry, saying, "By'r lay'kin! there was a honey-bee tangled in my locks."

And when he had sought for the bee to kill it with his hat, but could not find it, they did seat themselves again, he laughing and saying that "the bee was a bee o' much discretion and wondrous good taste."

That night when I crept to my little ladies to see that all was quiet, I, pausing in

the door-way, did note them as they lay—
my little lady with her head on Mistress
Marian's breast, and a smile on her lips,
and Mistress Marian with her arms wrapped
close about her, and her dark hair swept
out over the pillow, and thence to the floor,
like a stream o' water that reflects a black
cloud, but her eyes wide open, looking
straight forward, as though at a ghost.
And I stole off and sobbed myself to sleep,
but not before I had awakened Jock, who
did grunt, after the uncourteous, pig-like
manner of a suddenly wakened man, be-
thump his pillow as though 't had been an
anvil, and in turning over, twist the bed-
clothes half off of me, so that what with
the cold (it being then the fall o' th' year),
and what with my distress, I slept but un-
easily.

And the next thing I knew o' th' matter,
there was a wedding, and my little lady
wedded to Lord Ernle, and Mistress Marian her bridemaid. Surely if the good God

e'er sent happiness on earth, He did send
it to my little lady and to his lordship.
'Twas at this time that Sir Rowland asked
Mistress Marian to be his spouse. And
'twas even i' th' same spot where Lord
Ernle had discovered his love for my little
lady, that he asked her.

Again it was as though some one had
smitten her—her face deadly white and the
red line across her brow. She put out one
hand to keep him from her, and let it rest
on his shoulder, and she said, " Rowland, I
love thee well, but no man will ever call me
wife."

He said, " Is this the end?"

She said, " Though we should both live
to see the last day, it is the end."

Then he went, with his head bowed
down. And when he was gone, for the first
time in all her life she wept aloud.

Some time passed, and matters waxed
ever hotter and hotter 'twixt Cavaliers and

Roundheads, till one night there rode up a man to the castle gate with papers for Lord Ernle, and the long and the short o't was this : His lordship was ordered to ride forth to war, and my little lady only three months his wife. Now when this blow fell upon them they were all at meat in this very hall, for ofttimes in cold weather they dined here, even as thy father and mother do now, on account o' th' greater warmth.

And when my lord had glimpsed at the papers he did start to his feet, saying, " Where is the man who brought these papers ?"

Jock answered him, " He is gone, my lord."

Then snatching up a flagon of wine that was near at hand, he drank more than half that was in it. And again he turned over the papers in his hand. But all they, my little lady, and Mistress Marian, and your grandfather and grandmother, seemed turned to stone. All at once my little lady

started up as from a spell, and went and
got her arms about him, as in years gone
by when she had hurt him with his own
mock sword, and she cried out, "What is
it? what is it?" Anon came Mistress Marian to his other side, and looked over his
shoulder, while he stood between them like
one bewitched, and whiter than a man just
dead. When Mistress Marian noted the
contents o' th' papers, up went her hand to
her heart as on that day under the beech-
tree, and she caught at his arm to stay herself.

He turned from his wife to her as though
for help, saying, "Tell her, tell her, comrade." And he sank into a chair near by,
and dropped down his head into his hand.

Lord! Lord! that was a fearful night!
When they made my little lady to understand, she set up one cry after another,
each loud enough to pierce the very floor
of heaven. Ne'er since have I heard a
woman utter such cries as those. And no

one but Mistress Marian could in any wise appease her, for she would not have my lord come unto her, but drove him away with waving of her hands, saying, " Thou dost not love *me*, but the King! thou dost not love *me*, but the King!"

And when Mistress Marian sought to reason with her, 'twas even the same. Naught could she do but sit and hold her, and comfort her with soft words and noises such as mothers make o'er their young babes. By-and-by she was calmer, and asked to see her lord. So Mistress Marian went out, but I remained on a low stool at the bed's foot. Lord Ernle entered, and she crept into his arms like a fawn into the hollow of a rock when the hail is falling. And they clung to each other in silence. Presently he saith, " Darling, darling, that I should have brought thee to grief!"

She answered, " Nay, not thou, but God. O love, dost truly think that God is aye a good God?"

And he hushed and soothed her even more tenderly than did Mistress Marian.

Afterwhile she saith, almost in a whisper, " But thou needst not go?"

He said, " Darling, how dost thou mean?"

And she whispered more low and said, " I will go with thee to the new continent to-morrow, and there we can live the rest o' our days in peace and love." And she broke out all at once wilder than ever: " Ernle! Ernle! take me! I will go with thee! I will leave father, and mother, and home, and country, and friends, and King for thee! Only go not to war! go not to war!"

He said but two words back of his teeth, " I must!" and then again, "*I must!*"

But when he looked at her for answer, lo! she had swooned away.

He was to set forth in two days after the morrow; and on the morning of that day, behold! we could not believe our own eyes for astonishment when we saw the Lady

14

Patience step quietly forth, composed and gentle, though very pale. She saith good-morrow to every one, and after a while she doth slip her arm through her husband's arm, and saith she, "Come for a walk, Ernle; I have much to say to thee." So they started forth together. Now I, fearful of many things, did follow at a little distance. As they walked she besought him again that he would take her and set sail for the new continent. And when again he told her how that it could not be, she fell down upon her knees before him, and clasped him with her arms, and she said, "If thou dost not love me, let me be the first to die by thy sword. Slay me, as I kneel, for the love I bear thee."

He said, "Patience, Patience, thou wilt break mine heart."

And she, still kneeling, did cry out with a wild voice, "They lied who named me, for in an ill hour was I born, and I have not patience to support it! I thought that thou didst love me, and lo! thou lovest the husband of another woman more than thou lovest me!"

He bent to lift her up, groaning, but she would not; whereat he trembled from head to foot, and she shook with his trembling as the leaves of a tree when the shaft is smitten by lightning. And she cried out again, and said, "As there is a God in heaven, thou dost not love me, an thou canst go to war and leave me to die o' grief." Then, as though 'twas torn from him, he burst forth, "Now as there is a God, thou dost not love *me*, to torture me thus!"

And all at once she was quiet. So he stooped and lifted her, and called her his "bride," and his "wife," and his "darling," and his "heart's blood," and more wild, fond, foolish names than at this day I can remember. 'Twas near sundown, and that night he was to ride. Over against the dark jags o' th' hills there ran a narrow streak of light, like a golden ribbon. And the brown clouds above and below it were like locks o' hair made wanton by the wind, which it as a fillet did seek to bind. But they twain walked ever on, till by-and-by they neared that cave o' which I did tell ye. As they came in front o't my lady turned, and smiling piteously, "Ernle," saith she, "wilt thou go with me into the cave and kiss me there, that when thou art gone I may come hither and think o' thee?"

And he said, "Oh, my heart! what would I not for thee?" And he kissed her again and again.

Presently she said, "Do not think me foolish, but wilt thou enter first?—it is so dark." And she stood in the door-way, with her hand on the door, while he entered.

He said, "There is nothing here, sweet-heart, but a monstrous damp odor."

And she answered, "Nay, but go to the very end; there may be toads; and when thou art there, halloo to me." So she waited with her hand on the door.

He called to her, " There is nothing, love. Wait until I return to thee." But, ere he had ceased speaking, she clapped to the door with all her might, and did push forward the great iron bolt, so that he was a prisoner in the cave; I being rooted to the ground with astonishment, as fast as was ever the oak-tree under which I stood. At first he thought 'twas but one o' her pretty trickeries, and I heard his gay laugh as he came to the shut door, and he called out, and said, " So, sweetheart, I am in truth a prisoner o' war; but art thou not an unmerciful general to confine the captured in so rheumatic a cavern ?"

She sat down and leaned her head against the door, but said not a word.

And he spoke again, saying, " Darling, I pray thee waste not what little time doth yet remain to us."

Still she answered not; and again he spake, and his voice began to be sorrowful.

"Oh, my wife," he said, "canst thou jest at such a time?"

At last she answered him, saying, "I jest not."

His voice changed somewhat, and he said "What dost thou, then?"

She answered, "I keep what is mine. Where my forefathers did hide their treasure, there hide I mine."

He said, in a loud voice, "God will not suffer it."

Then fell a silence between them. But by-and-by he spoke again. "Darling," he saith, "surely thou dost not mean to do this thing?"

And she saith, like a child when 'tis naughty, and knoweth well that it is, but likes not to say so, "What thing?"

He answered, "Thou canst not truly mean to shut me here to bring dishonor upon me, who have loved thee better than man ever loved woman" (for so do all men say, and truly think).

She said, " Thy life is more to me than. thy honor."

And he groaned aloud, crying, " Oh God! that I have lived to hear thee say it!" and again there fell a silence, save for the whis- pering of the night in the trees above us and the creeping of small creatures through the dry grass. 'Twas almost curfew-time, and there was one star in the black front o' th' night, like the star on the forehead of a black stallion.

When he spake again his voice was very fierce, and he saith, " Patience, I do com-. mand thee to release me."

But she spake never a word.

And again he said, " Better let me out to. love thee, than keep me here until I. hate. thee."

She shivered, leaning against the door, until the big bolt rattled in its braces.

And he said yet again, " By the Lord God, an thou dost keep me here to. sully my good name, and that of thy father and mother, who have been to me even as my own flesh and blood, I will never live with thee again as man with wife, but will go forth into the New World to live and to die with thy handmaid dishonor!"

And she was silent.

Again he spoke, and lifted up his voice in a cry exceeding sorrowful and bitter, so that my heart froze to hear it.

"Woman! woman! was it for this I gave thee my fair fame to cherish? Or was it for this that I put my name into thy keeping? Oh, child, listen while there is yet time! Wilt thou with thy own hands take his manhood from thy husband to drag it through the mire? Patience, as I have shared thy childhood, as I have loved and cherished thy girlhood, as I have held thee in my arms as bride and wife, give me back my honor while there is yet time. Oh, my wife! my darling!" And I heard him sobbing like a little lad.

At that sound she put both hands over

her ears, and started to her feet, looking from right to left like a hunted thing, and I could bear it no longer, but leaped forward and fell on my knees before her, and grasped her kirtle with both hands. I could scarce speak for tears, but with all the strength that was in me did I plead with her to draw back the bolt, but she would not. Now to this day when I do think of the fool that I was, not to run without her knowledge and bring the old lord, thy grandfather, or bide my time and unbar the door when she had gone, it seems as though I must hate myself for evermore. But as I pleaded with her, all at once there was something cold against my throat, and I seemed to know that 'twas a dagger, and the steel cowed me, as it doth sometimes cow strong men, and I stirred not, neither spoke I a word more. Her face was over me, like a white flower in the purple dusk, but her eyes bright and terrible. And when she spoke, 'twas not my little lady's voice, but rather the voice o' a fiend. And she said,

"Swear that thou sayest nothing of all this to man, or to woman, or to child, else will I kill thee as thou kneelest."

And I knew that for the time she was mad, and would kill me even as she had said, did I not swear. So I did take that fearful oath, coward as I was, and to this day am I a craven when I think on 't. When I had sworn, she turned from me as though there were no such woman in all the earth, and went once more to the door o' th' cave, and called his name—"Ernle!"

He answered straightway, and said, "This once will I speak to thee, but if thou dost not unbar the door o' th' instant, I will never hold speech with thee again, nor touch so much as the hem of thy garments, by the living God!"

She said, "I cannot! I cannot! But oh! say not such dreadful words. We will be happy. 'Tis for that I keep thee here.

Speak to me! Ernle! Ernle! Ernle!
Call me thy love once more! Just once!
just once!"

But she might as well have plead at the
door o' a tomb for all the answer she got.
Again and again she called him, but a dead
man speaks no more than spoke her lord.
And at last she sprang to her feet, and rushed away into the darkness towards the castle, and I after her.

And when I was entered in by a side
door, and had changed my apparel and
gone forth to inquire after her, lo! she was
raving as with fever, and all they, her
father, and mother, and Mistress Marian,
thought that he had ridden away and left
her i' th' park, having said farewell to them
ere he and my lady did set forth to walk.
And they strove to comfort her.

The morrow was scarce dawned when she
was up and dressed, and stealing through
the covert to the door o' th' cave. I followed
her, for she heeded me no more, now that I

had taken the oath, knowing that I would be torn in pieces ere I would betray my trust. When she was come to the door, she kneeled down and leaned her head against it, and called to him, with a voice so exquisite low, 'twas almost as though one should hear the spirit when it speaks within, and she saith, " Ernle—my love—my love."

And all was still as death. And she said, " Darling, feel with thy hands for the bread and wine. It is near thee on the right o' th' door as thou enterest in. Two bottles o' wine and some loaves o' bread."

But he answered her neither by word or sighing. And she said, " Wouldst thou break my heart?" Then, when she saw that he would not answer her, she cast herself face down along the ground, and tore up the grass with her hands, and pressed down her face into the damp earth. And after a while (for th' looks o't) she rose and went back to the castle.

At nightfall there rode a man to the cas-

tle gate with papers, wherein my Lord Falkland did question wherefore Lord Radnor
had not answered the summons. And all
they were amazed and looked at one another. The messenger said, moreover, " If
that it cannot be proven ere to-morrow
night that the Lord Radnor hath been the
victim o' foul play, he will be branded as a
deserter throughout the land."

Thy grandfather gave one cry, " Murdered!" and the sound of it stilled the life
in me that I fell down as one dead. And
when I had once more come to the possession o' my wits, Jock did tell me as how
'twas already whispered in the village that
the young lord had deserted the cause, and
had set sail in secret for the New World.
Upon this, I straightway swooned again.
And when I was recovered enough to stand
upon my feet and go forth from my chamber, behold! there was a silence over all
the house, as in a house where the best be-
loved has died in the night.

Men scoured the country far and near, in search o' th' murdered body o' th' young lord. And 'twas now the evening o' th' third day. But my lady meant not to open the door until the morrow, for if she opened it ere then, she knew not but what matters might be righted, and her lord ride to the wars in spite o' all. When it was nigh to sunset she did creep forth and kneel at the door o' th' cave, and call to him in that beautiful, gentle voice, " Ernle ! Ernle ! my love ! my darling !"

And when he did not answer her, she ceased not, as on the day before, but went on: " To-morrow I will set thee free. As I live, thou shall be free to-morrow. An thou wilt but let me be near thee like thy dog, I will ask no more. Neither will I fret thee with my sorrow. Oh, love, I do beseech thee speak to me, whose only sin was in loving thee too dearly. Let the kisses that as a bride I have set upon thy lips plead with them that they speak to me. Oh, my heart! oh, my husband, have pity! If thou wilt never speak to me again, speak to me now. Say but my name, my silly, ill-bestowed name, ' Patience.' Nay, curse me, so I but hear thy voice. Call me what names thou wilt. In God's name, Ernle! In the name o' her who was once thy wife!" And as she knelt and pleaded as a woman with her God, behold! there stepped forth from the coppice Mistress Marian. She stood there like a figure cut in snow, for her kirtle was all of white sémé, and her hair was as a cloud fallen round about her. When she saw my lady she drew in her breath with a sharp sound, and set both hands against her bosom. And she bended forward from her loins and listened, but in none otherwise moved she. And my lady went on, " To-morrow I will set thee free — I do swear it. With the rising o' th' morrow's sun thou shalt be free as air. Only speak to me now. Only speak to me now. Just once, Ernle—just once."

With one spring Mistress Marian was upon her, and had pinned her arms to her sides. And the two women stood and gazed into each other's faces, with their throats stretched forward, as serpents stretch their throats ere springing upon each other.

Mistress Marian spake first, and her voice was as a voice that I had never heard, and she said, "So *this* is the truth, then?"

My lady said no word, but her eyes were aflame.

And Mistress Marian gazed on her for an instant more, then dashed her aside, and turned towards the cave.

"Ernle," she said, "take heart. I will set thee free—I, Marian!" But ere her hand did touch the bolt, my lady was upon her like a little tiger, and she wound her hands in Mistress Marian's thick tresses, and dragged her backward.

And they rolled over and over on the ground, even as do men when they fight, saying no word from first to last. The horror of it smote me that I fell down upon my knees and was dumb. Now my little lady was uppermost, now Mistress Marian. And had not my lady been strong with despair, Mistress Marian could ’a’ mastered her o’ th’ instant. But she fought like a she-wolf brought to bay, with teeth and talons too, and ’twas almost as though two of a size had fought there. Howbeit, with a sudden move, Mistress Marian flung my lady down, and set her knee upon her, and held her, and looked from side to side, as though at a loss, and my lady’s strength was fast failing.

When I saw that, I could bide still no longer, but ran forward, crying to Mistress Marian to be gentle with her.

She answered but these words, “ Nurse, take off my girdle and bind thy lady’s hands with it.” And there was that in her voice I dared not disobey. So I bound my lady’s hands, she saying never a word, and when the girdle was fast knotted, Mistress Marian helped her gently enough to rise, and bid-

15

ding me have a care o' her, turned and drew back the bolt from the door o' the cave.

The last light o' the sun fell like a golden lance across the threshold, and across my lord as he lay there, face down, with his hands against the sill o' th' door.

And she stooped down over him, saying, " He hath fainted for lack o' food," but I knew that there was both wine and bread i' th' cave. And she called his name, but he was silent. And she called him again and again. And at last she bade me come to her side, and when we had turned him upon his side so that his face was towards us, behold, he was dead. But Mistress Marian saith again, " He hath swooned away." And she put her hand upon his brow, but no sooner did she touch it than she cried out at its coldness, and shook the dead man in her frenzy, crying,

" Ernle! Ernle! thou art free! Wake, man! thou art free!"

I said, " Mistress, mistress, for love of God! Dost thou not see that neither thou nor any other can wake him more ?"

Thereat she fell back upon her knees, leaning upon one arm. And she said, " Dost thou mean—"

I bowed down mine head, for I could not meet her eyes. And she fell upon his body, and stirred no more, so that when they came to bear the poor young lord to the castle, they did bear her also. And for some hours we thought her dead.

Now when my lady saw them how they lay there, and the sunlight red upon them like to blood, she came and kneeled down in front o' me, and lifted up her poor fettered hands meekly, like a little child. And she said, " Nurse, I pray you tell me what it doth mean, for methinks I am waxing foolish, like poor Marjory i' th' village whose man fell from the cliff."

I could not answer her for sobbing.

And she said, " Do they sleep ?"

And I nodded my head, for I could say no word.

She said, " Pray you, do not wake them. An they sleep till the morrow, all will be well." Suddenly her wits came back upon her with a rush, as doth a wind that hath seemed to be gone for aye. And she snapt the girdle on her wrists like as it had been a thread o' silk, and ran and laid hold on him with her hands, and dragged him forth upon the grass. And she saith,

" Ernle! Ernle! Ernle! What! wilt thou not answer me, now that thou art free? See! thou mayest ride to war. It is not yet too late. What there, nurse! My lord's charger! Run! run!" Then leaped she to her feet with one cry that methought would 'a' cracked the welkin in twain above our heads.

" Dead! Oh God in heaven!"

So for an instant she stood, with her arms reached high above her head, and her eyes upon him as he lay at her feet, even as a flame doth poise for a breath ere sinking again upon the coals. But anon she dropped down beside him, and beat her forehead with the lower palms o' her hands, and she saith, "Well didst thou sign me with thy blood! well didst thou sign me with thy blood!" Then all at once did she peep up at me over her shoulder with one o' her winsome ways, and fell a-laughing softly.

"Nurse," saith she, "hath he not found a pretty way to punish me?   He feigns it well —by'r lay'kin—doth he not, nurse?"

And she rocked to and fro, as she knelt beside him, laughing softly to herself, and ever and again she would reach forth one little hand, all scarred in her struggle with Mistress Marian, and would touch a stray lock into place, and once she bent over and kissed him, laughing softly, and nodding to herself very wisely.   And she would sit that way, and rock herself to and fro, and smile upon the ground, and laugh softly, until the very day that she did die.   And the last words that she did ever say were, " Just once, Ernle—just once."

(Nurse Crumpet rises and stirs the fire, amid a heavy silence, broken only by the little Lady Dorothy's sobs and the rushing of the wind outside the great hall.)

THE END.

Woodfall & Kinder, Printers. 70 to 76 Long Acre, London, W.C.

Price 2s. each.

G. P. R. James.

Arrah Neil ; or, Times of Old.
Attila.
Beauchamp ; or, The Error.
Brigand ; or, Corse de Leon.
Castle of Ehrenstein.
Charles Tyrrell.
Dark Scenes of History.
Darnley ; or, The Field of the Cloth of Gold.
Delaware ; or, The Ruined Family.
De L'Orme.
False Heir.
Gentleman of the Old School.
Gowrie.
Heidelberg.
Henry of Guise ; or, The States of Blois.
Henry Masterton ; or, The Adventures of a Young Cavalier.
Jacquerie.
John Marston Hall ; or, The Little Ball o' Fire.
Leonora D'Orco.
Man-at-Arms ; or, Henri de Cerons.
Margaret Graham.
Mary of Burgundy.
Morley Ernstein ; or, The Tenants of the Heart.
My Aunt Pontypool.
Old Dominion : A Tale of America.
Philip Augustus ; or, The Brothers in Arms.
Richelieu : A Tale of France.
Robber.
Rose d'Albret.
Sir Theodore Broughton.
Stepmother.
Whim and its Consequences.
Woodman : An Historical Romance.

John Lang.

Will He Marry Her ?
The Ex-Wife.

George A. Lawrence.

Guy Livingstone
Maurice Dering.
Anteros. .
Sword and Gown.

Charles Lever.

Arthur O'Leary.
Horace Templeton.
Harry Lorrequer.
Charles O'Malley.
Jack Hinton.

Samuel Lover.

Rory O'More.
Handy Andy.

Lord Lytton.

Alice. Sequel to Ernest Maltravers.
The Caxtons.
The Coming Race.
Devereux.
Disowned.
Ernest Maltravers.
Eugene Aram.
Falkland ; Zicci.
Godolphin.
Harold, the Last of the Saxon Kings.
Kenelm Chillingly : his Adventures.
The Last Days of Pompeii.
The Last of the Barons.
Lucretia ; or, The Children of Night.
Leila ; Calderon ; Pilgrims of the Night.
My Novel, Vol. 1.
———————— Vol. 2.
Night and Morning.
The Parisians, Vol. 1.
———————— Vol. 2.
Paul Clifford ; Tomlinsoniana.
Pausanias ; The Haunted and the Haunters.
Pelham ; or, The Adventures of a Gentleman.
Rienzi : The Last of the Roman Tribunes.
A Strange Story.
What will He Do with It ? Vol. 1.
———————————— Vol. 2.
Zanoni.

GEORGE ROUTLEDGE & SONS, London, Glasgow, & New York.

Price 2s. each.

Captain Marryat.

Dog Fiend ; or, Snarley Yow.
Frank Mildmay ; or, The Naval Officer.
Jacob Faithful.
Japhet in Search of a Father.
King's Own.
Masterman Ready.
Mr. Midshipman Easy.
Monsieur Violet's Adventures.
Newton Forster.
Olla Podrida.
Pacha of Many Tales.
Percival Keene.   With Memoirs of Captain Marryat.
Peter Simple.
Phantom Ship.
The Pirate ; The Three Cutters. Memoir of the Author.
Poacher.
Poor Jack.
Rattlin the Reefer.
Valerie : An Autobiography.

Helen Mathers.

The Story of a Sin.
Jock o' Hazelgreen.
Cherry Ripe.
My Lady Greensleeves.
Eyre's Acquittal.

W. H. Maxwell.

Stories of Waterloo.
Brian O'Linn ; or, Luck's Everything.
Captain Blake.
Hector O'Halloran.
Captain O'Sullivan.
Stories of the Peninsular War.
Flood and Field.

R. Mounteney-Jephson.

Tom Bullkley of Lissington.
The Girl He Left Behind Him.
A Pink Wedding.
The Roll of the Drum.
With the Colours.
The Red Rag.

W. J. Nelson Neale.

The Pride of the Mess.
Will Watch.
The Port Admiral.
The Naval Surgeon.

Jane Porter.

Scottish Chiefs.
Thaddeus of Warsaw.

Mrs. Campbell Praed.

Affinities.
Zéro.
Moloch.
The Head Station.
An Australian Heroine.
Ariane.

Mrs. Radcliffe.

The Mysteries of Udolpho.
Romance — Italian — Udolpho, in One Volume.

Angus Reach.

Clement Lorimer.

Mayne Reid.

Afloat in the Forest. Perils in South American Inland Waters.
Boy Hunters ; or, Adventures in Search of a White Buffalo.
Boy Tar ; or, A Voyage in the Dark.
Bush Boys ; or, Adventures in Southern Africa.
Cliff Climbers ; A Sequel to " Plant Hunters."
Desert Home : or, The Adventures of a Lost Family in the Wilderness.
Fatal Cord : Falcon Rover.
Forest Exiles ; or, Perils Amid the Wilds of the Amazon.
Giraffe Hunters : A Sequel to " The Bush Boys."
Guerilla Chief.
Half-Blood : A Tale of the Flowery Land ; or, Oceola.

GEORGE ROUTLEDGE & SONS, London, Glasgow, & New York.

www.ingramcontent.com/pod-product-compliance
Lightning Source LLC
Chambersburg PA
CBHW020107030726
47498CB00006B/1989